Simon Grave and the Sons of Irony

Len Boswell

Black Rose Writing | Texas

First printing

This is a work of fiction. Names, characters, businesses, places, events, and incidents are either the products of the author's imagination or used in a fictitious manner. Any resemblance to actual persons, living or dead, or actual events is purely coincidental.

ISBN: 978-1-68433-621-0
PUBLISHED BY BLACK ROSE WRITING
www.blackrosewriting.com

Printed in the United States of America
Suggested Retail Price (SRP) $18.95

Simon Grave and the Sons of Irony is printed in Palatino Linotype

*As a planet-friendly publisher, Black Rose Writing does its best to eliminate unnecessary waste to reduce paper usage and energy costs, while never compromising the reading experience. As a result, the final word count vs. page count may not meet common expectations.

To all I love without condition,
To all I love without omission.

Never doubt.

Other books by Len Boswell

Simon Grave Mysteries:

A Grave Misunderstanding
Simon Grave and the Curious Incident of the Cat in the Daytime
Simon Grave and the Drone of the Basque Orvilles

Other Mysteries:

Flicker: A Paranormal Mystery
Skeleton: A Bare Bones Mystery

Memoirs:

Santa Takes a Tumble

Nonfiction:

The Leadership Secrets of Squirrels
Stick Figures: The Life and Art of Len Boswell

Simon Grave and the Sons of Irony

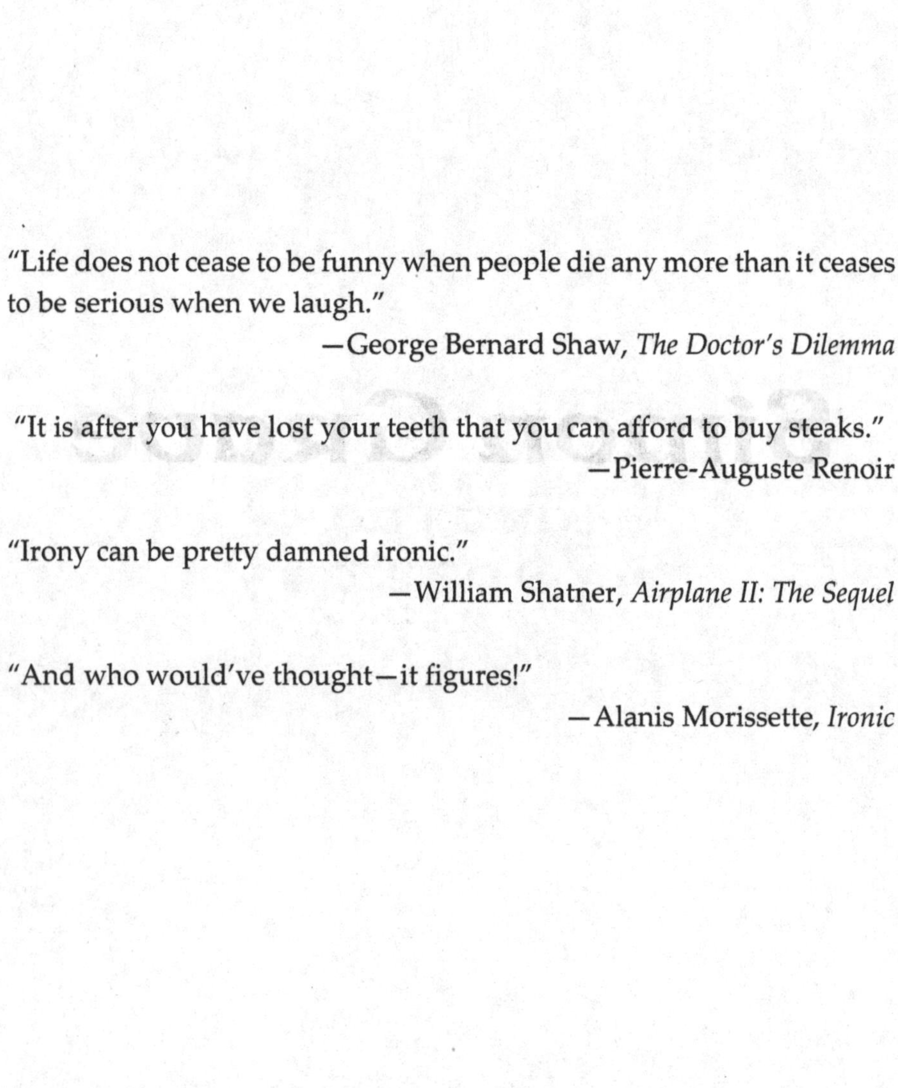

"Life does not cease to be funny when people die any more than it ceases to be serious when we laugh."

—George Bernard Shaw, *The Doctor's Dilemma*

"It is after you have lost your teeth that you can afford to buy steaks."

—Pierre-Auguste Renoir

"Irony can be pretty damned ironic."

—William Shatner, *Airplane II: The Sequel*

"And who would've thought—it figures!"

—Alanis Morissette, *Ironic*

1

Life can be ironic, death even more so. Or at least that's what Chase "Superman" Arnold, president of the Krypto Knights, was thinking as he pushed through the doors of the Sons of Irony clubhouse. He didn't know exactly what irony meant, but he knew it was at least clever and seemed to be as good a descriptor as any for what he was about to do.

No one noticed him at first. They were too busy playing pool and downing shots to notice that a rather large man in black leather cuts bearing the wrong club patch was standing among them, blood dripping from his sleeves and pooling on the floor.

Superman smiled wryly at the scene. It would be a fitting end, one his club would be talking about for years. The ballsyness of it. He would be a legend.

A man hunched over the pool table, cue poised to strike, suddenly caught his eye and looked up. Superman sniffed himself erect, gave him the broadest gotcha smile he could manage, winked, and fell face first to the floor, dead.

2

Captain Henry Morgan had seen many things in his 45-year career on the Crab Cove Police Force, but the events of the last few days ranked right up there with the strangest—and worst—in memory.

They had just wrapped up two related murder cases, the deaths of drone magnate Wright Orville and inventor Lachlan McLachlan, who had been conspiring in secret to launch a new technology—neural nodes and distributed intelligence, whatever the hell those were—to replace personal drones.

McLachlan's experiments had been at the heart of what the press was now calling *The Gull Conspiracy*. McLachlan, to prove his concept, had implanted a neural node into a local seagull and surgically altered the bird's voice box to give it the wonder of human speech. As it turned out, amplifying the gull's intelligence was a huge mistake.

The seagull, who had self-identified as "Horace" after his capture, had taken it upon himself to organize the local gulls to attack the drones that were dominating the air space around Crab Cove. As much as Captain Morgan loved his personal drone, Rum, he could appreciate Horace's point that drones made the life of a gull miserable. Their carefree days of gobbling up fallen French fries and harassing walkers on the boardwalk had been severely curtailed by a sky filled with drones.

The attack had been horrific, for drones and people alike. Captain Morgan had only to look out onto the squad room to see that. It looked more like a field hospital and drone repair shop than a highly functioning police department.

Detective Amanda Snoot and her new partner, Detective Polly Loblolly, who had been at the center of the attack, were covered in bandages, particularly their arms, which they had used to fend off the persistent strikes of the gulls. The EMTs had assured them that their wounds, though many, would not leave any significant scars. Tough and resilient, both had shrugged at the news. Now, just before dawn, as they began their shift, they were more interested in seeing what they could do to repair the many drones that had been incapacitated by the incident. Most were beyond repair, but some, including Loblolly's drone, Pine Cone, only needed a new rotor or two to be put back in service.

Captain Morgan knew that Sergeant Barry Blunt was somewhere in the room—his drone, Object, was hovering in a far corner—but the man was so damnably nondescript, so extra ordinary, that he was not easy to see, particularly if he was standing still. Charlize and Smithers, his simdroid detective team, who fancied themselves the equal of Sherlock Holmes and Watson, down to wearing realistic replicas of their Victorian clothing, were definitely not there; he had sent them out on another missing-cat case. Grave was there, of course, doing his best to interrogate Horace, who was tethered to Grave's desk. Not surprisingly, Retective Tilda Must hovered nearby, shadowing Grave's every move, waiting for her chance to interrogate him about his performance during the recent murders.

Captain Morgan looked on this scene with a growing sense that retirement was his only option. He was tired and burned out, and if he ever had a filter, it had long ago been blown off in tirade after tirade, usually for nothing at all. He was a man as wide as he was tall, which was considerable, with a neck as wide as his head, giving him a look, complete with crewcut, that most people would characterize as the look of a blockhead, not that anyone who valued their life would ever say that to him, even now. He had dark eyes, like a shark, and a nose that suggested blunt force trauma, the large blob of flesh near flattened to this face.

From what Captain Morgan could see, Grave's interview of Horace was proceeding apace, although contentiously. He wondered whether Grave was up to the task. That Horace was a smart one.

The beep from his drone distracted him. "How many calls, Rum?"

Rum seemed pleased at the number. "Thirty-seven, sir, a new record."

"Anyone important?"

"Both mayoral candidates, sir."

Morgan snorted. "Them? They can wait. Anything else?"

Rum buzzed for some moments. "A strange call, sir, from one Chase Arnold."

Morgan looked at the ceiling. "Chase Arnold, Chase Arnold, why is that so familiar?"

"Ah," said Rum, "you may also know him as Chase 'Superman' Arnold, of the Krypto Knights."

Morgan's eyes went wide. "Superman? Why on earth would he be calling *me*?"

"Well," said Rum, perhaps *too* matter-of-factly, "he was reporting his murder, presumably at the hands of the Sons of Irony."

Morgan leaped to his feet, as best as an aging champion of justice could manage. "Murder? Sons of Irony?"

"Yes, sir, at the Son's clubhouse. He said he'd be dead by the time you arrive."

"Holy mother of drones," said Morgan. "That's just, just—*unacceptable*."

Morgan started to move away, to gather up Grave for starters, but Rum stopped him. "Wait, there's more. He said since he couldn't reach you, he'd call the main station number."

Morgan glared across the room at the desk sergeant. "Then why in hell didn't I know this sooner?" He turned back to Rum. "From either of you."

Rum shrugged as best as he could manage without shoulders. "Sir, you said you didn't want to be disturbed and—"

Morgan waved him off, irritated. "Damnable hell!"

3

Clarence "Claw" Edwards, President of the Sons of Irony, proud member of the Men of Ahem, and one of the Bloody 9, looked down at the body with a mix of concern and glee: concern that they'd have to deal with the body, and glee that the president of a rival gang was dead. In his mind, images of burial sites competed with equally compelling takeover scenarios.

Claw was one of those men who appeared both tall and short. There was something almost simian about him. Up close, he would tower over you. But given some space, all you could focus on was how short his legs were. *Long strides* was not a term that could be used to describe the way he walked, which was more like a slow shuffle, and almost comical. Even so, he could freeze you with a glance from his near-black eyes. And if that weren't enough to cow you, his barrel chest and huge fists would do the trick. The tattoos running down each of his forearms spelled "Trouble," literally, the idea being that he was double trouble, which he certainly was.

"Well, well," he said. "Looky here. The once proud president of the Krypto Knights has met his end." He looked around the room. "Question is, which one of you idiots did this?"

Which one, indeed. He had six suspects: Oakley "Oakie" Kent, the oldest member; Manny "Andy" Kent, Oakie's son and best friend to Claw's son, Pax; James "Jerry Lee" Lewis, the club's Mallet Master;

Charles "Crabs" Morris, known for his scarred face; Bruce "Fid" Norman, who always seemed to be fiddling with something; and Pablo "Smoothie" Cruz, the only Latino in the club.

Claw looked them over once more. "Come on. If you did this, best fess up now."

Everyone either shrugged or threw up their hands.

"Not me," said Jerry Lee.

"Nor me," said Smoothie.

"Not none of us," said Crabs. "We were all here with you."

Claw looked around. "Where's Pax?"

Another round of shrugs and mystified eye rolling.

"Aw, shit," said Claw. "What, has that son of mine gone and done? He hated Superman."

"Aye, he did," said Fid, his hands moving through the air like a conductor. "But this is too stupid even for Pax."

"Right," said Andy, stepping forward. "Pax is my best friend, and I know he didn't do it. He's out courting that new doctor at the hospital."

Claw gave Andy a knowing smile. "Yeah, that's more like my son." He looked down at the body again. "Wait, where's my old lady?"

"Sookie's in the office, Claw, like always," said Crabs. "Working on the books, both sets, for the last couple of hours. She couldn't have done it, either."

Claw puffed out his cheeks. "Who then?"

Oakie cleared his throat to get Claw's attention.

"What?" said Claw.

"Think about it," said Oakie. "The president of a rival club has received a death wound. He knows he's going to die. He could drop on the spot, of course, but he could also show up here. Make it look like we killed him."

"Yeah," said Claw, "that makes sense, in an ironic sort of way, but why?"

Oakie shrugged. "I don't know. Maybe to cover up the identity of the real killer. Maybe another Knight did it."

Claw nodded. "It's a contentious club. I could see that."

Fid jumped in. "Or maybe who killed him isn't important at all. Maybe he just wanted to get us. You know, for revenge."

Oakie laughed.

"What?" said Claw.

"I was just thinking," said Oakie. "You're right. Him showing up here and dying is pretty ironic, at least from his point of view."

Claw cocked his head. "Ironic, eh? Well, maybe, but whatever." He looked around the room. "Where are the prospects? We need some shovel work done"

"They're on a spice run," said Smoothie.

Claw shook his head. "Well, then, I guess two of you will have to do the deed."

Fid and Jerry Lee raised their hands, but Andy spoke up. "Wait a minute. I have a better idea."

4

It was a dark and stormy night in much the same way that it was a bright and sunny morning, meaning that among all the things on the mind of Detective Simon Grave, weather was at the very bottom of the list. And why not? If you're sitting at your desk at the station with a talking seagull going on and on about the unfairness of his arrest, most things in life would drop to the bottom of any list. Even worse, the bird, who identified himself as "Horace," seemed to have a better command of the English language than Grave.

"The implant alone is exculpatory evidence," said Horace. "I mean, I was *non compos mentis* during the incident. You must see that."

Barry, Detective Grave's personal drone, gave out an appreciative whistle as he hovered above them. Detective Grave, for his part, just nodded with as serious an expression as he could manage and pretended to write an important note, but it was really just a doodle of a bird hanging from a noose. "Uh-huh."

He was trying his best to focus on the interview, one of the last details of the Basque Orvilles murder case, but the sight of Retective Tilda Must pacing just outside the interrogation room distracted him. She wanted to get him in that room and do a deep dive into his methods and actions in the case—to retect what he had detected. Yes, it was her job, and there was none better at it than Tilda Must, a simdroid constructed to resemble the late actress Tilda Swinton, in her youth of course.

"Excuse me," said Horace, "but are you paying even the slightest attention to what I've been saying?" Horace didn't know quite what to make of the man interviewing him. This Detective Simon Grave was tall and square-jawed to be sure, and held his chin skyward, suggesting both arrogance and innate innocence, or to Horace's advanced mind, perhaps low intelligence. His eyes were blue in the way that the sky was blue on a brisk winter morning, and yet gray in a way that clouds were gray before a storm, when gulls best find shelter. His nose was strong and prominent, with a little speed bump in the middle. His lips were thin, like fine cut French fries, but with a pinkish hue, and his hair was as thick and black as the hot tar in a parking lot on a summer's day.

Horace tried again, raising his voice to the next level. "Hello, Earth to detective."

The bird's voice startled Grave. "Um, of course. Now, you were saying, about this distributed intelligence thing."

The bird cocked his head. "No, I was not saying that. I was asking when I could get some cold French fries, preferably from the boardwalk, with a soupçon of malt vinegar, hold the ketchup. Old Bay would be good, of course, but again, not too much."

"Oh," said Grave. "Well, there'll be time enough for that once we've finished up here."

"It would help speed things up if you paid attention."

Grave glanced over at Retective Must. "Of course. Now, then, why is it that your creator—"

Horace screamed. "Not creator. *Surgeon.*"

Grave nodded. "Okay, why is it that your *surgeon* selected you for his experiment with neural nodes and distributed intelligence?"

"Me specifically? I have no idea."

"I mean, why not select a parrot or some other bird with the ability to mimic human speech?"

"Ah, I see what you mean. Well, to be frank, he was terrified that no one would believe him if he implanted his neural node into a bird that could already talk. People would just think it was a trick."

"I see what you mean. So he chose you instead?"

"He lived on the beach. We seagulls are everywhere, and we're always hungry. So he just held up a handful of French fries, and that was that. The next thing I knew I was in a cage in his laboratory, being prepped for surgery."

"For the implant."

"Yes, but the implant was the easiest part. He knew just where to attach the electrodes. The hard part was his work on my voice box."

"So you could talk like you're talking now."

"Indeed." The bird looked around. "Are we done here? I'd really like to be going."

Grave looked over at Retective Must, who gave him a steely look and tapped on her watch. "Um, just a few more questions."

The bird rolled his eyes. "Very well."

"Now, what was the purpose of this experiment?"

Horace gave him an exasperated look. "What, we've already gone over this."

Grave had no memory of any such thing, but knew he'd been distracted enough by Retective Must's looming presence to miss a freight train rumbling through the station. "Just to be clear."

Horace sighed. "Okay, *to be clear*, first comes the implant, what Lachlan McLachlan called a neural node. A simple device, really. Intended mostly to replace drones as far as communications are concerned, and with a full knowledge base equivalent to and perhaps surpassing the latest simdroids."

"So we'd receive calls in our heads instead of being relayed through our personal drones."

"Exactly. And that's the easy part. His plan was to use the neural nodes as his moneymaker, a means of funding his research on distributed intelligence."

"That being?"

The gull shook his head. "You really weren't paying attention, were you?"

Grave shrugged and tried not to look sheepish, but failed.

"Okay, then," said Horace. "You're familiar with octopuses, I assume?"

"Octopi?"

"*Puses* is preferred."

"Octopuses then. What about them?"

Horace sighed and looked around the room. "Is there nothing to eat here?"

"No, nothing at all," said Grave. "Now, as to the octo, um, puses."

"An octopus distributes its intelligence. Did you know that each of their suckers operates independently but cooperatively with the other suckers?"

"All right, so?"

"So what McLachlan wanted to do was to extend brain function throughout the human body."

"So, if someone cut off a man's head, the rest of the body would continue to function?"

Horace nodded. "Exactly, and may I say, the military saw the advantages of that immediately."

"I see, I see." Grave flipped back to his earlier notes. "Now, you said you were one of *two* gulls in McLachlan's laboratory. What happened to the other one?"

Horace rolled his eyes. "Okay, for the second time, the other gull was named Arnold, and he was stolen by someone in the night, shortly after McLachlan's murder. I have no idea who, but I do know that McLachlan would have been very upset about it. He thought Arnold had taken to the neural node better than I had. Not true, of course, as you can plainly see from my high level of functioning."

"But you escaped this man?"

Horace spread his wings as if to say, *look, here I am*. "As you can plainly see."

"And then you organized the attack on the town."

Horace snorted. "Not on the town, on the drones." He gave Barry a menacing look. "They don't belong in the sky."

"So you say."

"Yes, indeed I do."

Grave was about to ask whether the military had funded McLachlan's research, but he couldn't help noticing his boss, Captain Henry Morgan, rushing toward him, eyes wide.

"Grave, into my office. We might have another murder."

Grave leaped to his feet and motioned for his drone, Barry, to follow.

Horace squawked. "Hey, what about my French fries?"

The driverless police hovercruiser sped through town, its computers changing traffic lights from red to green as it picked up speed, the outside world becoming a multicolored blur, like a child's finger painting. Somewhere in that painting was Crab Cove itself, a small seaside town dedicated to all things crab. If they had been moving more slowly, the painting would have revealed crab shacks, tee-shirt shops, and a steady stream of brightly clothed tourists, each followed overhead by their personal drone.

Detective Grave was not a fan of driverless vehicles, so he tried to ignore the blur and focus on the face of his boss, Captain Harry Morgan, which itself had become a blur of sorts, its once chiseled features now a landslide of wrinkles and drooping flesh. "Sir," said Grave, "What's this all about?"

"I received a call from Superman, as did our desk sergeant."

Grave chuckled. "Superman? You mean like *Superman* Superman? Clark Kent?"

"Don't be stupid," said Detective Amanda Snoot, who was sitting next to the captain. "Don't tell me you've never heard of Chase "Superman" Arnold, president of the Krypto Knights hovercycle club?"

Grave gave her a blank look and shrugged. Snoot was not among Grave's favorite colleagues, even though her performance of late had been stellar, particularly her work on the Orville-McLachlan murders.

Maybe it was her appearance that put him off. Everything about her was pinched. When she looked at you, she squinted in a way that suggested you were some low, barely sentient entity not worthy of her presence. Her one patented response to everything, good or bad, was to screw up her tiny mouth in lemon-sucking disdain. Thin as a rail, with a head too large for her body, she looked like a walking doorknob, a doorknob with rust-colored short hair cut both long and short, as if she had been sheared this way and that by a mischievous child.

And now she was squinting at him again.

"Jeez," she said. "How can you *live* in this town and not be up to speed on our hovercycle gangs?"

"They ride in parades, right?"

Snoot rolled her eyes. "Holy mother of morons, Grave. The Sons of Irony, the Krypto Knights, the Vie Kings, the SanniClaws, these gangs are the dark undercurrent of Crab Cove, and have been for years."

"Ah, yes, the SanniClaws. They ride in the Christmas parade, right?"

Captain Morgan jumped in. "Listen to her, Grave. She's absolutely right, and her knowledge of these clubs is why I brought her along. She was once a member of one of the clubs."

That didn't surprise Grave. From her penchant for wearing nothing but black, to her close-cropped hair, to her sneering attitude, she would have fit right in with a gang.

Captain Morgan turned to Snoot. "Which one was it again?"

"The Prickly Pairs," said Snoot.

"Pears like fruit?" said Grave.

Snoot gave him a smirk. "No, pairs like pairs. Couples. You know, a man on the hovercycle and his old lady in the sidecar."

Grave gave her an appraising look. "You in a sidecar? I can't picture that."

"Which is why that arrangement didn't last too long. Still, I learned a lot about the clubs in this town."

"And we'll need that knowledge," said Captain Morgan. "As I was saying, or *trying* to say, I got a call from Superman. He said we would find his body at the Sons of Irony clubhouse."

Grave opened his mouth to say something, then changed his mind and closed it.

"Yes," said the captain. "It's a headscratcher."

Grave resisted the temptation to scratch his head. "So he's self-reporting his murder?"

Snoot rolled her eyes. "You catch on fast, don't you?"

Grave ignored the slight. "So, Ms. Gang Expert, tell me about the Sons of Irony. What are we walking into?"

Snoot took a deep breath and launched into the story of the Sons. The hovercruiser sped on, the colors swirling.

A story should not be rushed. There must be room for proper pacing, embellishment, and details—all the things that make a story fulsome and memorable. As it was, with the hovercruiser in headlong flight to the Sons of Irony clubhouse, Detective Snoot felt rushed. She was sure she had left out many important details, but the time available was what it was.

She had told them that the Sons of Irony hovercycle club had been formed in 2048, shortly after Claw defected from a now defunct club, The Merry Punsters, in New Pennsylvania. Claw had grown weary from the constant stream of puns required to get through a day at the Punsters clubhouse. So, with his share of the cash from a recent crabmeat heist, he had climbed on his hovercycle and driven till the sun went down. And that is how he ended up in Crab Cove, sleeping behind a dumpster outside the Red Crab Laundromat, Dry Cleaners, and Ironry.

The word *ironry* made him laugh; it wasn't a word at all. And yet maybe it should have been a word, because it certainly would describe an establishment in the business of ironing. *Ironry, a place for ironing,* he thought, and laughed again. *And maybe, maybe,* he thought, *this would be the perfect front for my new club, the club I would build from nothing, to launder money from the operations of other hovercycle clubs.*

It was almost ironic, he thought. *Or maybe it wasn't.* He wasn't sure. At any rate, a few conversations and a pile of cash later, the laundromat was his. His first act was to change the name of his new company to Red Crab Steamers, and its nature from laundry and dry cleaning to food trucks specializing in steamed crabs. He sold off all the washing machines and dry cleaning equipment, gutting the building to make way for food operations and an expansive clubhouse for his new club, which he dubbed in an homage to the previous establishment the Sons of Ironry.

That name lasted as long as the first order for the club's leather vests, or what they called *cuts,* when the patch maker, sensing a clear typographical error, changed Ironry to Irony. Claw could have asked for a redo, but everyone seemed to love the name, so it stuck. It was perhaps the only thing ironic about the club.

Detective Simon Grave had interrupted at this point, asking about the club's illegal activities and how they got away with it with apparent impunity.

Captain Morgan had an answer, albeit an unsatisfactory one. "They've been under surveillance for over a year now. The problem is, they've got twenty food trucks scattered all over Crab Cove, each with their own food routes. To catch them at anything would require hundreds of officers, all operating in concert."

"So the money laundering goes on unabated?" said Grave.

"Exactly," said Snoot. "Now, can I get back to the story?"

"Wait a second," said Morgan. "Grave, we suspect more than money laundering. They move bushels and bushels of steamed crabs, along with packs of picked crabmeat. The thought is they may be transporting other things with the crabs. Guns perhaps, or drugs."

Snoot shook her head. "I was getting to that."

"Speaking of getting places," said Grave. "We seem to be slowing down."

Morgan turned and looked out the rear of the hovercruiser, searching for the drones, Barry and Rum. Any other day, he would have looked for Snoot's drone, Goth, as well, but Goth had been torn to pieces just days ago during the Orville-McLachlan murder case, and Snoot had still not found a suitable replacement.

The two drones were in hot pursuit of the hovercruiser. Barry was in level flight, but Rum was waggling back and forth.

"Looks like I have an urgent phone call," said Morgan.

Grave and Snoot peered through the back window and nodded.

"It does," said Snoot with a sigh. "I do wish Goth was here."

Grave was not good at empathy. The best he could do was make a recommendation for a new drone. "I hear the Apple 37s are quite the rage."

Snoot smirked. "No personality. Too quiet. I want a drone you know is there. Has to make a little noise, you know what I mean?"

"Speaking of making a little noise," said Morgan. "We're here. Time to roust out a murderer, make a little noise of our own."

The hovercruiser floated to a stop amid a fleet of Red Crab Steamer trucks, each featuring a large, three-dimensional steamed crab that rotated at various speeds to get the attention of hungry workers and tourists. The air was filled with drones, some menacing security drones, some personal drones, and some delivery drones, all various versions of flying crabs.

7

First impressions were everything, or at least they were something important, at least to Detective Simon Grave. In his experience, innocent people were first encountered going about their business and not congregated in a tight, arms-crossed crowd trying to stare you down and intimidate you. Their personal drones, each a red flying crab, hovered menacingly, mechanical claws clacking.

Even Captain Morgan was taken aback by their greeting, this wall of silence and animosity. He would have said something, but his drone, Rum, was waggling to beat the band, trying to get his attention. Morgan nodded at Snoot and stepped back toward the hovercruiser to take whatever call Rum was so frantic about.

Taking his cue, Detective Snoot strode up to Claw and poked a finger in his chest. "Where the fuck is the body?"

Claw looked left and right at his men, then turned back to Snoot with a sly smile. "And what body would that be, detective?"

"Superman."

Claw laughed, then turned to his men and encouraged them to do the same. "Any of you guys see Superman fly in? Maybe Clark Kent?"

"Very funny," said Snoot. "We're looking for the body of Chase 'Superman' Arnold, president of the Krypto Knights."

Claw smirked. "Oh, him. Well, detective, you know our club's do a smattering of business together, all legit of course, but really, there's no love lost between us. But as much as it pleases us to hear of his death, I assure you we had nothing to do with it—*nothing.*"

"Right, right," said Snoot. "Well, we'll have a look around if you don't mind."

Claw shrugged. "Be my guest."

"No, wait," said a distressed Captain Morgan, walking up. "That won't be necessary. It seems the body has been spotted at the clubhouse of the Vie Kings."

"Wait, what?" said Grave. "Superman himself said his body would be here."

"Oh, right," said Morgan, looking confused.

"Let me get this straight," said Claw. "You got a call from a dead man?"

"Yes, that's right," said Snoot. "Said he'd be found right here." She turned to Captain Morgan. "And not at the Vie Kings."

Claw shrugged. "I guess another caller disagrees. So, search if you must, but to my mind, you best talk to the Vie Kings, not us. They hated him even more than we did."

Snoot and Grave turned to Morgan for guidance.

"We're already here, so we'll look around," said Morgan. "I'll call the station and have them send Charlize and Smithers to the Vie Kings."

Claw was shaking his head. "A waste of time, captain, but have a look-see. We have nothing to hide."

Now it was Snoot's turn to laugh. "Oh, right, right. A gathering of innocents is what you are."

Claw feigned offense. "Detective, detective, you wound me to the core."

Snoot rolled her eyes, then pushed her way through the gathered Sons. If there was a body here, she'd find it.

8

Harold "Bluetooth" Mortenson, president of the Vie Kings, was having a hard time coming to grips with the fact that the body slumped on the Vie King's intricately carved throne was that of Chase "Superman" Arnold. A despised member of the Krypto Knights.

Confused, Bluetooth turned to Pokie. "How, when, *what* does this mean?"

Filip "Pokie" Sigurdsen, club vice president and resident pagan priest, or *hofgothi,* a man on a first-name basis with the gods, stroked his scraggily red beard.

"As Odin said in the *Hávámál, a guest is in the hall. Where shall the stranger sit down? Why, to make a new friend, quickly give him the bench nearest the fire."*

They were certainly in the hall, or at least the Quonset hut that served as their mead hall, longhouse, and clubhouse. And the fire was indeed close by, but Pokie's words were irrelevant to the situation, causing Bluetooth to roll his eyes. "The man is dead, Pokie. He's neither a guest nor welcome."

The two men were a study in contrasts. Where Bluetooth was tall and broad and Viking-like from head to toe, Pokie was small and frail and, as his name suggested, slow, both in movement and aptitude. Bluetooth had blue eyes, Pokie brown. On it went, small nose to big nose, thin lips to plump lips, blond hair to red hair, big hands to small hands, and so on. A Viking and a mini-Viking, if you will.

Pokie poked at the body. *"Bury the bodies of the fallen when you find them in your travels, whether they be killed by disease or drowned in the sea, or slain on the field of battle."*

Bluetooth huffed. "Stop with your religious babble. I want to know what *you* make of this, not Odin."

Pokie shrugged. "If we didn't kill him, someone else did, and they're trying to get us to take the fall."

As slow as Pokie was, he was not altogether stupid, and had an uncanny way of simplifying even complex problems. This skill made him indispensable to Bluetooth and the Vie Kings, who as a group tended to be less bound to logic. "Well, what are we to do?"

"We could bury him, I guess, but think a moment. Who would set us up like this?"

Bluetooth considered the possibilities. "I can only think of two possibilities: the Sons of Irony or the Krypto Knights themselves."

"Why would the Knights kill their own president?"

Bluetooth looked down at the body. "Everyone hated this man, even his own club."

"So you think it was them?"

"Could be, but it could also be the Sons. They'd like nothing more than to see us take the fall, so they could move in on our spice operations."

Pokie nodded and stroked his beard. "Perhaps, but is placing the body here on our throne ironic enough for them? They love their little ironies more than I love even Odin."

Bluetooth considered the possibilities and grew more confused. "There are so many possibilities."

"Enemies may array themselves in battle, but to survive, you must first choose one and only one among them to strike."

"Indeed," said Bluetooth, "but we must also take care to deflect suspicion from our own swords."

Pokie nodded. "What would you have me do?"

Bluetooth chuckled. "Get the men, and quickly. I have an idea worthy of Odin himself."

Pokie smiled. "Tell me."

"When we're on our way. Come, let's get the van."

"For the body?"

"Yes, and find my drone. We'll need to call the police along the way."

"The police?"

"Yes, Pokie, we'll need to time this just right. We'll want the body to be discovered as soon as our work is done."

Pokie nodded, a smile growing on his face. *"No one can keep anything concealed once it is heard in the hall."*

"Yes, something like that," said Bluetooth. "Come on, let's go. We're losing darkness."

Charlize and Smithers, Crab Cove's up-an-coming simdroid detective team, received Captain Morgan's call shortly after their debriefing on the latest missing-cat case. Retective Must had been her thorough self, and Charlize had been more than willing to go into great detail, from the scraggily appearance of the cat, to the details of its disappearance, to its eventual capture, the result of exquisite logic, forensic science, and established police procedures and protocols.

"You make us simdroids proud," said Must.

Charlize smiled. "We can't help it. We're just programmed that way."

While Must resembled the young Tilda Swinton, Charlize was a dead ringer for the young Charlize Theron, and Smithers looked exactly like Lawrence of Arabia himself, the young actor Peter O'Toole, albeit with the voice of Richard Burton, an idiosyncrasy demanded by his first owner. Of course, he was a free simdroid now, as was Charlize, and he could pursue his greatest desire: to be Watson to Charlize's Sherlock Holmes.

"Shall we go, then?" said Smithers.

Charlize was already pushing back from the table. "Yes, time, as always, is of the essence. To the Duesenberg."

She was of course referring to their custom, electric-powered 1929 Duesenberg Model J, a vehicle Charlize had built from a kit, thinking it just the right vehicle for a modern-day Holmes and Watson. It combined the look and ample accommodations of a carriage, complete with decorative landau irons, with the muscle, flow, and sparkling chrome that came with a new century, albeit the early twentieth century.

As they moved through the squad room, Charlize noticed the captured seagull, Horace. Something about the bird intrigued her, and it was not just Horace's ability to converse intelligently. She had the feeling that he was a clue somehow to a crime greater than coordinating an attack on the town's many drones.

She would have liked nothing more than to interrogate the bird right then and there, but Captain Morgan needed her at the clubhouse of the Vie Kings. Horace would have to wait.

Horace noticed them leaving the station and called out. "Hey, babe, how's about you get some French fries for me on your way back. I'm starving."

Charlize and Smithers smiled politely at Horace and continued out of the station and into the waiting Duesenberg, Charlize issuing orders to the car. "Clubhouse of the Vie Kings, shortest path, full speed, full sound."

The car was equipped with an utterly quiet electric motor, but Charlize had recently modified its programming to simulate the throaty rumble of the Duesenberg's original straight-eight internal combustion engine.

They sped away, Charlize still thinking about Horace, and Smithers combing his databanks for anything related to the Vie Kings.

10

Grave, Snoot, and Morgan were being worked by the Sons of Irony, and they all knew it. A Son had been assigned to shadow each of them. Captain Morgan was being shadowed by Claw himself, while Detective Snoot drew the attention of Crabs, who followed her into the clubhouse.

Grave decided to stay outside. If a body was dropped off here, there might be drops of blood or perhaps an unusual tire track or hover track. Even hovercycles left distinctive swirls in the dirt. A good forensic technician could tell you the make, model, and engine details, even the weight of the rider. Beyond blood and swirls, there might also be other things: string, cigarette butts, matchbooks, and a world of sundry items that occasionally get left behind at a murder scene.

His shadow, Jerry Lee, followed his every step, hovering at his shoulder, quietly humming a Jerry Lee Lewis song. Jerry Lee's drone, Elvis, provided background instrumentals. It was like karaoke for hummers. Grave's drone, Barry, seemed to like it; he hovered and waggled to the beat.

"What's that you're humming?" said Grave.

"It's *Breathless*, by Jerry Lee Lewis. Gonna sing it tonight at the Legion Hall. If you have time, you should stop by. We get to wailing around midnight."

Grave considered the invitation. "Um, sorry, not a fan. I'm more into gospel."

"Gospel? Shit, I would have never thought."

Grave nodded. "I get that a lot. But, the thing is, I just love it. You should, too. It's at the root of rock and roll."

Jerry Lee suddenly laughed. "Wait, are you the insane dude who drives that little red Austin Healey Sprite around town with the radio cranked up to eleven with gospel music?"

He was, and he sensed a complaint would be coming next.

But it wasn't. "That is so cool. I mean, not the music. Gospel's for churches, not me. But the outrageousness of the sound. By god, it makes me feel good that an outlaw like you is out there, thumbing your nose at our quiet little town."

Grave frowned. "I'm not sure that outlaw is the right term, but it's true I like gospel, and I like it loud. It helps me think."

"Really? Well, if it helps, I can sing any Jerry Lee Lewis song for you as loud as you want."

Grave considered the offer and shook his head. "That won't be necessary."

Jerry Lee shrugged. "Suit yourself."

They walked along in silence until they came upon a row of black hovercycles. All bore the crab logo of the Red Crab Steamers company, but each was tricked out in different ways.

"These your hovercylces?" said Grave, asking the obvious question.

"Yeah, by day we use them to deliver special orders of crabs to local restaurants."

"Really? I thought you used delivery drones for that?" He looked into the sky, which was filled with them.

"Oh," said Jerry Lee, "yes, we do, but some of the orders are too big for our delivery drones."

Grave cocked his head. "All right, but what about at night?"

Jerry Lee blanched. He had somehow trapped himself without realizing it. "Oh, oh, well, at night they mostly just sit here, or we drive them home."

"But don't you use them for club business as well?"

Jerry Lee shook his head. "Club business? No, I mean yes, I mean club business is mostly delivering crabs, so there's occasionally a late-night request for more crabs. Some of these beach parties get crazy, right?"

Grave pressed him further. "As I recall, you also ride these in the daily Chamber of Commerce parades."

Jerry Lee sensed he was near an escape from this line of questioning. Certainly, there was nothing more benign than riding in a parade. "Yes, yes, absolutely, we're upstanding, civic-minded men. We do our part to make Crab Cove what it is today."

"And what's that?" said Grave.

Jerry Lee shrugged. "Um, Crab Cove?"

"Yes," said Grave, "Crab Cove is Crab Cove."

Grave turned and walked down the line of Harley-Musk hovercycles, letting his hand fall on the metal cowl over each of the hoverengines. They were all warm to the touch.

He turned back to Jerry Lee. "So, any crab deliveries today?"

Jerry Lee shook his head emphatically. "Nope, we've been in meetings all morning, assessing the damage from the gull attack. We held our own, for sure, but you can imagine the interest a flying crab would have for a seagull."

Grave smiled and began humming *Breathless*.

"Damn, you hum good," said Jerry Lee.

11

Charlize and Smithers sat quietly for a time; they both enjoyed riding in the Duesenberg, with or without the added faux rumble of the engine. Even at high speed, the Duesenberg seemed to glide along. If it weren't for the scenery buzzing by, the car would have felt like it was standing still.

Smithers felt compelled to comment on it. "Have you noticed that when the car is parked it looks like it's speeding?"

Charlize was in deep thought, trying to analyze what they knew of the case so far—a body seemed to be moving around Crab Cove—so she was a bit startled. "What? Oh, yes, it's the design. Designers had more say back then."

"And yet, here inside, we seem to be at rest."

"No surprise. It was designed for absolute comfort, a luxurious parlor on wheels."

"I'm so glad you built this for us."

Charlize gave him an acknowledging little grunt.

Smithers knew what that meant; she wanted to change the subject. "So, what do you make of the case?"

"A little too soon to say, although it has at least one intriguing element."

"The body."

"Yes, or rather the lack of a body—so far."

"Did Captain Morgan say who directed us to the Vie Kings?"

"An anonymous call, per usual."

"And may I assume the first call, directing him and Grave and Snoot to the Sons of Irony clubhouse was also anonymous?"

Charlize chuckled. "That's where it gets interesting, Watson."

More and more she seemed to prefer calling him Watson instead of his real name, Smithers. At first, Smithers had corrected her, but now he realized it was just her way of getting into character. "How so?"

"It seems the supposed victim, one Chase "Superman" Arnold, president of the Krypto Knights, called in his own murder. Told Captain Morgan and the desk sergeant they'd find his body at the Sons of Irony clubhouse."

"Odd, don't you think?"

"Odd, I do think. And my first thought is that our Superman was seeking revenge or payback for something."

Smithers nodded. "What research I've been able to do suggests that all these clubs exist in a strange hate-tolerate relationship. They hate each other, but know they must cooperate at times to reach their goals."

"Speaking of research, what do we know about the Vie Kings?"

"Well, first of all, it's the smallest hovercycle club in Crab Cove. Just six members, primarily because proven Scandinavian heritage is a requirement for membership."

"I see."

"Not that that was always a requirement. The name of the club caused some confusion at first."

"What do you mean?"

"The club was formed way back in 2046, in Ocean City, Maryland, by a woman named Violet King."

"Ha," said Charlize. "Vie Kings is a play on her name, then?"

"Yes, exactly, although it had an apostrophe back then: Vie *King's.*"

"Interesting. Why not Vie's Kings?"

"I don't know. Perhaps that apostrophic version suggests the club members were more than they were. You know, kings. The other way around, Vie King's, means the club's power is in her hands, apostrophically speaking. Anyway, it was a unisex club, and popular, with some forty members. But events overtook the club. The drowning of Ocean City by the rising Atlantic Ocean made them flee to Crab Cove, and then Violet died in the Covid-47 pandemic, the last pandemic before the discovery of the Univaccine. Anyway, that caused a power struggle within the club. Long story short, the women left and Violet's second in command, Harold "Bluetooth" Mortenson, took over."

"And dropped the apostrophe for another play on words, Vie Kings as in Vikings."

"Yes, and then he purged all non-Scandinavian members."

Charlize nodded, then slumped back into her seat and folded her arms in thought. "Hmm, okay, so what do the Vie Kings do for money, and what's their relationship with the other clubs?"

Smithers looked out the window. The Duesenberg was slowing to a stop in front of a Quonset hut that served as the Vie King's longhouse. "I have some information about that, but perhaps we can ask them directly. We're here."

12

The Sons of Irony were as consistent in their farewells as they were in their greetings. As Morgan, Grave, and Snoot piled back into their hovercruiser, the Sons assembled in a line again, arms folded, defiant as ever.

Morgan had found nothing. Snoot had found nothing. But Grave, for his part, had found a clue. "They're lying."

"Lying?" said Morgan.

"Yes, Jerry Lee said they'd been in meetings since dawn, but all their hovercycles were warm to the touch."

"So you think—" said Snoot.

"Yes," said Grave. "I think the body was here, but they moved it."

"To the Vie Kings?"

"Yes," said Grave. "No love lost there, and the Vie King's clubhouse is the closest."

"So," said Snoot, "they're playing hot potato with the body."

Morgan shook his head. "But why? I mean, if they're innocent, why not just report the body and let us do our work?"

"That would have been the smart thing to do," said Snoot. "But these clubs follow their own brand of logic. And it seems clear, at least to me, that for whatever reason, they don't want the police to focus their attention on them."

"I don't know," said Grave. "Aren't they always under our scrutiny?"

"They are," said Morgan. "We have them under routine surveillance." He sighed. "Of course, it's never enough."

Snoot nodded. "And I'm sure they're aware of it. When I was with the Prickly Pairs, we'd laugh about such surveillance. Go about our business, all the while carrying out our plans right under their noses. No, what's going on here is not a fear of routine surveillance. Something big must be in the works."

Morgan seemed taken aback. "Big?"

"A transaction," said Snoot. "A big one. Big enough to make them worry about undue attention."

"Makes sense," said Grave. "And it may also mean that they're off the hook for this murder. I mean, why draw attention to yourself when a big deal is going down?"

Morgan nodded. "Right."

"No," said Snoot. "We need to consider them suspects. If there's one thing I learned as a club member, it's that plans go astray and—"

"Shit happens," said Grave.

"Speaking of which," said Morgan, pointing to Rum, who was waggling to indicate an incoming call. "Another call."

He beckoned Rum forward. "Who is it this time?"

"Well, sir, "I'm not sure you're going to believe this."

"Go on," said Morgan. "Try me."

13

Charlize and Smithers stood outside the Vie King's "Longhouse," a rusty but long Quonset hut that apparently once served as a garage. The last ghostly traces of a business sign, "Mike's Garage," ran in an arc across the top of the hut in faded red paint, just above double garage doors firmly rusted shut. The only entrance seemed to be a door to the left of the garage doors, suitably adorned above it by a horned helmet. Two hovercycles, each with a carved wooden prow out front, like a serpent prow of a Viking ship, were parked by the door, a horned helmet on the seat of each.

"Looks like at least two Vie Kings are at home," said Smithers. "Shall we go in?"

"Yes, no, wait." She walked over to the hovercycles and placed her hand on each. "Warm, almost hot. They've been doing some traveling, at speed."

She lifted each helmet and ran her finger around the inside rim. "Sweat. They've only just arrived." She sniffed at the helmets. "And they could both use a good bath."

"But no body," said Smithers. "Unless it's inside."

Charlize shook her head. "I think we'll find only excuses here, Smithers. If the body ever was here, and I suspect it was, it is certainly long gone now. But perhaps, through deduction or induction, whichever serves, we can determine why the body was diverted here of all places."

Smithers nodded, but not with any firm grasp on what Charlize had just said. She tended to be obscure at the beginning of a case. "So, we go in?"

"We go in." She stepped forward and knocked on the door.

The door opened quickly, perhaps too quickly, a small red-haired man peering out at them with beady brown eyes.

"At every doorway before you go in, look around you and watch out; it is hard to know where a foe may lurk; he could be standing before you," said the man, whose voice was high but strangely gravelly. "So said Odin, and so says I. Be you foes?"

Charlize shook her head. "We are neither foes nor friends, but seekers of truth and justice."

Pokie cocked his head. "Your words seem godly. Are you a follower of Odin?"

"No," said Charlize, "we are followers of leads. In this case, we are looking for leads that might help us find a body said to be here."

"Here?" said Pokie. "There's nobody here."

"Perhaps not," said Charlize, "but we are committed to searching these premises nonetheless."

Pokie's eyes went wide. "Premises? We have no *premises* here."

Charlize wondered whether the man was really this dense. "No, sir, what we mean is we need to look around inside your clubhouse, to see if there's a body."

"Oh," said Pokie. "That's different. By all means come in. We have nothing to hide on our, what you called it, premises. A funny word. It hisses like a snake when you say it."

Charlize nodded. "Yes, it does."

Pokie realized he was blocking the way, and jumped back. "Oh, do come in. My name is Filip Sigurdsen, but you can call me Pokie. I'm the club's *hofgothi*. What you might call a priest or spiritual adviser."

"I am Detective Charlize Holmes and this is my assistant, Doctor Smithers-Watson."

Pokie nodded, and waved them into the clubhouse. "Welcome, then."

Nothing could have prepared them for what they were about to see. The exterior to the building may have been faded and rusty, but the inside was as grand as any Viking longhouse ever was. The walls were lined with rough-hewn logs, and furs seemed to be draped on everything. An open fire blazed at its center and beyond that sat a large man upon a carved wooden throne, a Viking-themed drone, complete with tiny horned helmet, hovering above him.

"Welcome," said the man. "My name is Harold Bluetooth Mortenson, president-king of the Vie Kings, but you may call me *Harold* or *Bluetooth* or *Harold Bluetooth* or simply *your majesty*."

"Um, yes," said Charlize, holding a hand to her ear. "I will do just that, but first I have an incoming call. If you don't mind, I will step aside and take it. Won't be a moment."

She motioned at Smithers. "My assistant, Doctor Smithers-Watson has a few questions for you in the meantime."

Harold Bluetooth looked puzzled. "But I see no drone. How could you take a call?" And then it hit him. "Ah, I should have known. You are simdroids. How wonderful. And if I am not mistaken you are patterned after a famous actor."

Charlize nodded. "Yes, I was made to look like—"

"No, don't tell me," said Harold Bluetooth. "It's Heather Fleece, right? Am I right?"

"Um, no," said Charlize. "I'm—"

"No, wait, I'll get it. Yes, yes, of course, you're modeled after Dolores Fitzwatson, the British actress from some years back. The likeness is uncanny."

Charlize shook her head. "No again."

"Really? Wait, then. Just give me a minute."

"Fine," said Charlize. "I'll just take this call." She turned to Smithers. "Please proceed."

Smithers nodded as she walked away. She wanted to get out of earshot before she had to deal with Captain Morgan. She had already guessed why he was calling.

14

Bruce "Brush" Langley, Crab Cove's chief sanitation engineer and president of the SanniClaws Hovercycle Club, ran a tight ship, or rather a tight garbage truck. His world may have been trash and garbage, and all the screaming gulls, rotting crabs, and pulsing maggot masses that came with it, but he would tolerate nothing less than a clean and spotless clubhouse. Drop a crumb and you were in trouble. So the sudden appearance of a ripening corpse on the front porch of his clubhouse was not something he took lightly, or silently.

At six feet five and two hundred and fifty pounds, he was an intimidating man, even in the club's white-trimmed red jumpsuits, a nod to the pun within their name. Every day was Christmas to Brush and his boys, but today's gift was far from welcome.

"What's this?" he screamed, flapping his arms at his sides as he turned to club member after club member, looking for an answer. "Who done this?"

All he got from the club was a chorus of "NOT MEs" and "DUNNOs." Even their drones, which were designed to look like little flying elves, waggled in the negative.

Jimmy "Mr. Bucket" Furlong, the club vice president, a bald man a head shorter than Brush, leaned down and looked at the corpse's face. "Holy refuse, it's Superman."

Lionel "Bags" Mixon, the club secretary, and the Nelson Twins, "Trash" and "Garbage," the clubs new prospects, agreed.

Brush shook his head. "Makes no sense, him being here, dead and all. We've got nothing against the Krypto Knights. Do good business with them."

"Maybe he was coming to see us, and someone jumped him," said Mr. Bucket.

"Not likely," said Bags. "There'd be more blood. Look, the blood on his clothes is near dry. No, this happened someplace else."

Brush nodded. "I think Bags is right. Someone killed him and then dropped him here. But why?"

"Had to be another club," said Trash Nelson.

"Yes, another club," said Garbage Nelson. The twins seemed to agree on everything, as if they shared a mind between them, and sadly, half a mind for each. Brush wasn't sure they'd ever be anything but prospects.

"So, what do we do?" said Bags.

"Put him in the landfill," said Trash Nelson

"Yes, the landfill," said Garbage.

"No," said Brush. We didn't do this, and it's clear, like Bags said, Superman was killed somewhere else and then dropped here. What we do is what any upstanding citizen of Crab Cove would do."

"Put him through a wood chipper and toss the bits into the bay?" said Mr. Bucket.

Brush rolled his eyes. "Of course not. We call the police."

"Wait, wait," said Bags. "We can do our duty, all right, but there's another way, a way that will save us a world of trouble." He knew his boss well, and added, "And it will make the mayor look bad."

Brush brightened. "Come on, let's go while it's still dark."

15

Sergeant Barry Blunt was happy to receive Captain Morgan's call. He had had his fill with the chaos at the station, and was more than eager to go out on assignment, as was his drone, Object. Detective Polly Loblolly and her drone, Pine Cone, on the other hand, took some convincing. She was more interested in repairing the drones that had been dented and mangled by the seagulls.

"Are you sure he wants me to just drop everything?" she said to a space nearby, where she hoped Sergeant Blunt was standing. Unlike most of the team, she was still having a hard time laying eyes on the man, who was so nondescript he may as well have been invisible.

"Over here," said Blunt, his voice coming from an unexpected direction.

She turned quickly, zeroing in on the sound. "Well? Well? Are you sure he wanted me specifically? It sounds like anyone could do this."

Blunt nodded invisibly, then realized he'd have to speak. "Yes, he was quite specific. He wants me *and you* to go to the clubhouse of the SanniClaws, to find the body of Superman."

Loblolly laughed. "Superman? What, are you playing games with me, Sergeant?"

"No games," he said. "I'm talking about Chase "Superman" Arnold, president of the Krypto Knights Hovercycle Club, now believed to be dead." He hesitated. "But missing."

Loblolly cocked her head. "Missing?"

"Yes," said Blunt. "It's a long story. I'll fill you in on the way."

Loblolly sighed and put down the drone she had been working on. "I'll be back, little fellow. You'll be right as rain."

The drone made a soft beeping sound.

"Seriously," said Loblolly. "I'll be right back. You just rest here with your friends."

"Come on," said Blunt. "We need to move, now."

Loblolly stood and followed what she thought was a man-sized cloud across the squad room. If her memory was correct, she'd have to say he was a classic cirrostratus cloud. Of course, cirrocumulus was also a possibility.

As they left the station, a certain tethered seagull cried, "French fries, dammit!"

16

Captain Morgan had been a man of eminent patience once, but no more. Advancing years and the drumbeat of retirement had made him among the most impatient men on the planet. He wanted a body, now.

Grave was skeptical of his plan. "Sir, are you sure about this?"

This was a plan to divide and conquer. He had sent Sergeant Blunt and Detective Loblolly to the clubhouse of the SanniClaws, the next logical drop point for this game of body hot potato. He didn't suspect them in the least; they were government workers, sanitation experts, with a clean and spotless record. Hell, they even marched, or rather hovered along, in the daily Crab Cove parade sponsored by the Chamber of Commerce to attract and delight tourists and travelers who wanted a little fun before they departed for the Mars Colony from the newly built launch facility just outside the city limits.

That would allow the rest of them to converge on the clubhouse of the Krypto Knights, the most logical next best place to be, at least according to Morgan's logic.

Detective Snoot was more in Grave's camp. "Sir, Superman said his body would be found at the Sons of Irony. Why would he be at his own clubhouse?"

Morgan grunted angrily, his next words coming through clenched teeth, a sure sign that Patience was no longer in the hovercruiser.

"Because, de-tec-tive, because his fellow club members are his family, and who do we suspect first in any murder?"

Snoot sighed. "The people closest to him, his spouse or other family members."

"Or?" said Morgan, waving his hands impatiently.

"His fellow club members," said Snoot, completing Morgan's logic. "Still—"

"Still *nothing*," said Morgan, slapping his hands down on his knees to signal the end of alternative logic.

They grew silent for a time, images of Crab Cove swirling past the window as the hovercruiser reached maximum speed.

"Sir," said Grave finally.

"What?" Morgan's tone suggested he was still at the boiling point.

Grave would have to be careful, and calm, not force things. "Nothing, really, just a thought."

Morgan sighed a sigh that was loud enough to create an echo, had a canyon been handy. "What then?"

"I'm coming around to your way of thinking, sir."

Morgan's eyebrows almost launched off his face. "You what?"

"Yes, sir, I think you're on to something."

Snoot suppressed a laugh. "Oh, this should be good."

Morgan's stare silenced her.

"Go on," said Morgan.

"Well, sir," said Grave. "Let me be Superman for a moment."

Snoot snickered, Morgan silencing her again with a look.

Grave continued. "I've been wounded, by whom we don't know yet. The killer has apparently left me for dead, thinking the deed was done."

"Yes, so," said Morgan, wondering if Grave was on a different, unauthorized logical path.

"So, put yourself in his place. What are his options?"

"Call for help," said Morgan.

"Yes, either 911 or maybe someone in his club."

"But he doesn't do that," said Snoot.

"No," said Grave. "He calls you, sir. He calls you first. You specifically. Not 911, not the hospital, not his fellow members. He calls you, sir. *You.*"

"So?" said Morgan, not quite following Grave's logic.

"Well," said Grave, "that's part of the puzzle. For some reason he heads to the clubhouse of the Sons of Irony, and for some reason, he thinks you and you alone are the best person to follow up on this information."

"I don't follow," said Morgan. "Why would he do either?"

"I'm not sure either, sir. But it seems to me, there's a link we're not seeing, a link that suggests Superman—our dying Superman—wanted you to take the lead. That only you would understand why he decided to die at the clubhouse of the Sons of Irony. He dies there for a reason, and he thinks you'll know why."

"Aw, hell," said Morgan, scratching his head, "I don't know nothin'."

Snoot resisted the chuckle that was building at the back of her throat. "Sir, I think Grave is onto something."

Morgan sighed. "Maybe. Let me think on it."

The hovercruiser began to slow, blurs becoming fractals, fractals becoming images, images becoming monsters standing in front of a building marked "KK."

17

Blunt chuckled despite himself. Detective Polly Loblolly was clearly having an anxiety attack, much like Grave did every time he rode shotgun with him. "I'm here, really."

She looked at him, or hoped she was looking at him as the old hovercruiser sped down the Third Coastal Highway, heading for the Crab Cove Landfill and Recycling Center, home of the SanniClaws Hovercycle Club. Driverless hovercruisers were bad enough, but this ride with a near invisible driver had her pumping invisible brakes on the passenger side. "I'll get used to it. I know you're there." She squinted just to make sure. "Aren't you?"

He had to laugh. "Yes, yes, I'm here. Don't worry, I have a better driving record than our fleet of driverless squad cars."

"Well, I hope so." She began lightly tapping on the brakes as they approached an intersection at speed. She was sure the light would change and they would be T-boned by a thirty-six wheeler.

He glanced over at her. "Tell you what. If you stop pumping the brakes, I'll let you drive on the way back to the station."

She threw her head back and laughed. "Deal!"

Blunt drove on, occasionally glancing over at her. He was a happily married man, but he knew a beautiful woman when he saw one. She was tall and blonde and buxom, with an earthy girl-next-door beauty and a disarming smile. She was a new addition to the force, and to

Blunt's mind, a welcome one, and not just because of her beauty. She was a good detective with a great record at her previous place of employment, the now submerged state of Delaware.

She caught him looking, or thought she did. There was something less cloudlike about him. In her youth, she had delighted at seeing images in the clouds. This one a bird, that one a train. But now, the one looking at her seemed to have taken on the shape of a fox or maybe a wolf. "What?"

"Nothing."

She shrugged and looked ahead. "Are we there yet?"

"Almost. We'll take a right up ahead there, and then drive maybe a mile to the landfill."

"Eww, I can't wait for the smell."

"Oh, I wouldn't worry about that. Bruce Langley, the head honcho there, runs a tight ship. Scent neutralization and enhancement techniques have come a long way. The last time I was out here, the place smelled like a floral bouquet."

"Well, maybe there'll be the smell of a dead body this time."

Blunt chuckled. "Yeah, but I wouldn't put money on it. Captain Morgan thinks the body is at the Krypto Knights. You and I are the Just-in-Case Squad."

"So this is just a waste of time?"

"Maybe. Probably. Of course, the captain is wrong most of the time."

Loblolly laughed. "I'm beginning to realize that."

Blunt pointed up ahead. "There she blows."

The gates of the landfill were wide open, not unusual for this time of day, but Blunt could see right away that no one was manning the little checkpoint house and that the parking lot at the main office was empty.

"Damn, looks like nobody's home."

He pulled up as close to the office building as he could, parking in a space reserved for Langley himself. "Let me just check the front door."

"Okay, you do that, and I'll scoot over to the driver's side."

He laughed. "Now I'll be the one pumping the brakes."

"No you won't. I'm a good driver."

"We'll see." He handed her the keys, got out of the car, and walked up the sidewalk to the front door.

When he saw the note taped to the door, he stopped, threw up his hands, and walked back to the hovercruiser. "I should have known."

"Known what?"

"It's almost nine."

"So?"

"So, the SanniClaws will be riding in the daily parade."

"That tourist thing?"

"Yeah and the SanniClaws are pretty much Crab Cove celebrities. Everyone loves their costumes."

"Given their name, I'm guessing they dress up like Santa Claus."

Blunt chuckled. "You'd be half right. They're part Santa Claus and part crabs. Really, claws and all."

"Weird."

"Yeah, but the kids love them."

Loblolly sighed. "So what now? Should we catch up with the others at the Krypto Knights?"

Blunt returned the sigh. "No, let's head on over to the parade route, talk to them when it's over."

She shrugged. "Sounds good." She nodded in the direction of the passenger seat. "Hop in."

Blunt walked around to the passenger side and got in. "Ready when you are."

She waggled her eyebrows at him, threw the cruiser into gear, and sped out of the parking lot, the headlong speed forcing Blunt back into his seat. He tried stepping on the brakes, to no avail.

18

The snallygaster, a beast part dragon, part bird, and part octopus, stared out at them, its expression fierce, its intention clear. Had it been anything more than a painting on the side of a building, they would have been in trouble. Or maybe not. Painted just above the snallygaster was a seven-pointed star, providing mystical protection from that very same snallygaster.

"I don't get it," said Captain Morgan. "What has this thing got to do with Superman and the Krypto Knights?"

Detective Snoot, an expert on all things hovercycle gangs, had a ready answer. "It's a play on their name, sir, at least the Krypto part. Replace the *K* with a *C* and you've got *crypto,* and from there you jump to the club's two prime interests: cryptology and cryptozoology."

"Cryptozoology?"

"Yes, sir, as in cryptids, mythical beasts, the stuff of legend, folklore, and hoax."

Morgan nodded. "You mean like bigfoot."

Snoot sighed. The captain just didn't get it. "No, sir, bigfoot is a recognized primate, discovered in 2037, I believe, along the Snake River Canyon, in Idaho."

"Oh, right, right," said Morgan. "I remember now. A whole colony of them."

"Yes, sir, and now a protected species."

"Wait, wait," said Morgan, his memory trickling back. "Didn't they teach one of them to speak English?"

"Um, no sir. Sadly, bigfeet don't have the right voice box for articulated speech."

"Is that so?"

Grave, who had been distracted by another painting, one of the Catman of Wicomico County, perked up at *voice box*. "Well, now that someone has given a new voice box to a seagull, we should be seeing speaking bigfeet soon enough."

Morgan grunted agreement, then looked at his watch. "Where the devil are Charlize and Smithers? They should have been here by now."

The three of them turned away from the paintings and stared back at the approach road to the Krypto Knights clubhouse.

Nothing.

But then the unmistakable sound of the Duesenberg grew louder and louder, the car finally coming into view and speeding to a gravel-spraying stop in front of them.

Charlize was the first out, and wasted little time. "Where's the body?"

"Not sure, we were waiting for you," said Morgan.

"You shouldn't have done that, sir."

"No," said Smithers walking up beside her. "Time is of the essence."

"Indeed," said Charlize. "Particularly with this elusive body." She caught sight of the paintings. "What's this?"

Snoot turned back to the paintings. "Snallygaster. Catman. Couple of Maryland cryptids."

"Yes, yes, I know," said Charlize, "but I would have thought there'd be a painting of Chessie, the most famous cryptid, a creature of the Chesapeake Bay, said to look like Nessie of Loch Ness, in Scotland."

"Ah, yes," said Snoot. "By rights there should be, because the Krypto Knights shield, the one you'll see on the back of their cuts, is dominated by a writhing Chessie."

Captain Morgan had had enough of all things cryptid. They had work to do. "Well, shall we?" he said, pointing at the front door to the clubhouse.

Everyone nodded agreement and moved to the door.

Morgan turned to Charlize. "I'll take the lead if you don't mind?"

"Not at all, sir," said Charlize. "I'd love to see your legendary investigatory skills in full display."

Morgan was a bit taken aback. Was she messing with him? No one had ever described him that way. Not once in his entire career. Still, he went with it. "Yes, watch and learn."

But there would be no watching or learning. No sooner had he raised his hand to apply a legendary knock upon the door then his drone, Rum, buzzed beside him. "Phone call, cap'n."

Morgan could only sigh. And as for the others, they could only let their crests fall. There would be no body here.

No body at all.

19

There are parades and then there are parades. Some are grand, like the annual Mars Day Parade, but on just another Tuesday, the parades amount to little more than a traffic jam of costumed, unenthusiastic marchers watched by a small crowd of parade watchers who figured, what the hell, let's watch the parade.

Not that this parade wasn't different in one respect on this particular Tuesday, one week before the mayoral election. Along with the Crab Scouts Marching Band, the Chamber of Commerce Welcome to Crab Cove float, the Ramrod Robotics "Into the Future" float, the Crab Cove Cinema Cemetery's "Wonderland of Memories" float, a host of children and their drones dressed up like crabs, and a v-formation of SanniClaws hovercycle riders and their drones celebrating all things crab and Christmas, there were two noteworthy additions to the parade: Maura Lee Bancroft (*You can bank on Bancroft!*), the incumbent mayor, and her challenger, Lester Change (*Let's Change with Les Change!*), the first simdroid to ever stand for an election.

As each candidate and their fixed smiles and waving arms passed by in convertocruisers, the crowd responded with a smattering of polite applause. Even Detective Loblolly and Sergeant Blunt got caught up in the controlled excitement, applauding as each candidate drove by.

"It's going to be a strange election," said Loblolly.

"Why do you say that?"

"Come on, a simdroid running for office?"

Blunt shrugged. "They hold down regular jobs now, just like Charlize and Smithers, so why not?"

Loblolly shook her head. "I don't know. I mean, they're not *human*."

Blunt was surprised by her apparent bias. "You're not one of those simdroid haters, are you?"

Loblolly's steely look suggested an emphatic no. "Of course not. It's just that . . ." She let the words hover in the air.

"Just that *what?"*

Loblolly sighed. "Well, they're not *human."*

"You said that already."

Loblolly shrugged. "I know."

"Look," said Blunt, "my wife, June, works at Ramrod Robotics and has been involved in the development of simdroids from the get-go. She says simdroids, particularly their new candidate-series models, are more human than humans."

"I hear you, but it just doesn't seem right that simdroids can even vote, let alone run for office."

"Well, you can lay that at the feet of history. The Supreme Court's Citizens United decision set the stage for it."

"Right, right. Don't tell me. I'm familiar with the logic. People are people, but companies are also people, and if companies are people, their products are people, too. At least if they're deemed sentient. No voting rights for semi-sentient toasters and the like, of course."

"Exactly," said Blunt. "The law says we're all equal."

Loblolly nodded. "I hear you, Blunt. But still, it kind of gives me the creeps. I mean, what if Ramrod and other companies flood the world with more and more simdroids just to increase the vote count for simdroid candidates. And what if those same companies exercise complete control over the elected simdroids? I mean, it's scary, Blunt."

The cloud that was Blunt seemed to roil. "No, it won't be like that. There are too many controls for that to happen."

She shook her head. "I don't know. I think I'll vote for Bancroft."

Blunt, aghast, started to say something, but then stopped himself. Loblolly was new to the area and couldn't be expected to know the level of corruption within the Bancroft Administration. And she clearly wasn't up to speed on the candidate-series simdroids like he was, the result of many kitchen-table discussions with June.

Blunt surveyed the parade. "Look, here they come, right behind the Cinema Cemetery float."

Loblolly craned her neck to see over a group of tourists. "Right. What's the plan?"

"We'll follow them to the end of the parade. There's a parking lot where the marchers turn in and then disperse."

"Sounds good."

"Look," said Blunt. "See the guy at the tip of the v-formation? That's Bruce Langley, the club president. They call him Brush."

"So, we'll start with him?"

"Exactly."

As the formation of hovercycles approached, Blunt's drone, Object, began to waggle in the air.

"Looks like you've got a call," said Loblolly.

"I'll just take it as we walk along. Could be June."

They began walking down the sidewalk, keeping pace with the SanniClaws formation. Their pursuit did not go unnoticed by Brush and the other SanniClaws, who turned their heads as one and gave Blunt and Loblolly crab-eating grins.

20

There are medical examiners like Jeremy Polk, humans schooled in the arts and sciences of medicine and forensics, who are then confronted with case after case, each requiring diligence, exquisite attention to detail, and nuanced introspection, sometimes to the point of following hunches and a well-oiled gut. And yet, if you passed him on the street, you would think him wholly unlike your image of such a man, save perhaps for his arrogance.

He was a small man, but held himself in a way that suggested a much taller small man. It was his posture—back rigid, chest thrust out, head tilted to one side, chin up, nose high, lips curled into an arch snarl, one brow higher than the other—that suggested he might be almost an inch taller than he actually was. The effect was so startling that your first reaction was to look down at his feet to see if he was on tiptoe, which he never was. He had a big nose and beady, close-set eyes, which would level on you, fix you in place as he revealed the results of his work on a body, his hands either wildly waving in the air to make a point, or gripped together, like he was wringing a cloth to get the last drop out. His hair, once jet black, was now white and thinned to the point of wisps, not unusual for a man of sixty-seven years.

Yes, there are medical examiners like Jeremy Polk, but there are also medical examiners like the ME-4350 Forensic Analyzer Array, a new suite of ME equipment foisted on Polk by the mayor and the city council after being foisted on them by the International Space Commission. It was needed, the ISC said, because of the town's close proximity to the Mars Terminal. Any accidents that might occur there, said the ISC, would require state-of-the-art forensic capabilities far beyond those generally available to a town as small as Crab Cove.

And, since it was provided at no cost to the town, the mayor and the council quickly accepted the gift. "Gift" did not necessarily mean the ME-4350 was "gifted," at least in Jeremy Polk's mind. He had his doubts, so he had delayed using it, making up excuse after excuse to rely on his own expertise and not that of the dreaded machine.

From a practical standpoint, the first step in using the new ME-4350 was to place the body in a body delivery pod, or BDP, to assure clean transfer of the body from the scene to the entry port of the ME-4350. Once inserted into the delivery port, the body would be conveyed from analyzer to analyzer, each focused on a specific segment of the investigation. Clothes would be stripped off and submitted to every forensic test known to man or machine. Every square inch of the body would be photographed, medically scanned, and washed, the wash water itself subjected to no less than a hundred tests. Solids in the wash water—tissue, hair, dirt, and so on—would also be analyzed through a long series of tests. And as those tests were being done, body fluids would be withdrawn from the body and subjected to even more tests.

Then the body would move on to the gross and micro segmentation stations, where things like wounds would be studied in detail. Such an exam could not just tell you that the victim had been shot with a 9mm bullet, but also give you angle and depth of entry, estimated distance from gun muzzle to entry point, and so on. And if knife wounds were present, the machine could tell you angle and depth, likely sequencing of stabs, and the force required to inflict the wounds.

Given this information, the ME-4350 could then provide an animated simulation of the crime, showing the would-be killer inflicting his death wounds. It could then match the murderer's method of operation (MO) to known perpetrators in the ME-4350's crime database. A list of likely suspects could then be generated for follow-up by authorities.

All Jeremy Polk could do as this process unfolded was to sit in the viewing theater with Captain Morgan and the others, and try to look intelligent.

"It's kind of like a Rube Goldberg machine," he said. "It does things I can do easily, but in maddeningly complex ways."

"Oh, no," said Charlize. "If my databank serves, it's just the opposite. A Rube Goldberg machine, named after cartoonist Rube Goldberg (1883-1970) is a machine designed to perform a *simple* task in an indirect and overly complicated way. The intricate array of machines before us, on the other hand, has been designed to perform complex tasks in a decidedly direct way."

Polk smirked at her. "Whatever. My point is that I could do the same tasks just as well."

Charlize grunted. "I think that remains to be seen."

"Fair enough," said Polk.

"And," said Grave, "you know what I always say about tools."

Captain Morgan new exactly, and didn't want to hear it again. "Yes, yes, Grave, we all know. Now could you please—"

But Grave would not please. "If the only tool you use is a small wooden mallet, every problem looks like a steamed crab."

Captain Morgan cleared his throat with as much force as he could manage. "Someday you'll have to explain that to me, Grave." He turned back to Polk. "But for now, Polk, may I ask a question?"

Polk, who had been glaring at Grave, turned to Morgan and nodded. "Of course."

"If you don't like this machine, why are you using it?"

Polk sighed. "I don't, and I didn't. The body was already being processed when I arrived this morning."

"What?"

"Yes, someone had put the body in a pod and loaded it into the delivery chute. By the time I showed up, the process was well underway."

Charlize smiled. "Wonderful. If we're right about the travels of this body, there should be evidence from each of the club's locations, as well as DNA evidence directing us to whomever touched the body along the way."

Polk frowned and shook his head. "I'm afraid not, detective, though you were perfectly right to think so. But no, the initial readings and analysis from the first stages of processing suggest the body was naked and thoroughly—and I mean *thoroughly*—washed before it even went into the pod."

Charlize was taken aback. "Washed? Not a single clue?"

"Nothing," said Polk. "I can show you the readouts if you wish, but really, there's nothing."

Snoot spoke up. "Wouldn't that suggest the last person to handle the body is our killer?"

"That would make sense," said Captain Morgan. "If you're innocent, why would you go to the trouble of washing the body?"

Sergeant Blunt, who was somewhere in the room, had another thought. "I agree, and the sequence of events suggests strongly that the murderer was from the last club in the chain, a club known for cleaning and sanitation."

Captain Morgan didn't like the way this was going. "Wait, you can't seriously think the SanniClaws did this. Why, they are upstanding citizens, and great friends with the mayor." He turned and tried to locate Blunt, who seemed to be hovering in the far corner, barely visible. "How did they react when you confronted them?"

The voice of Sergeant Barry Blunt replied somewhat sheepishly. "We didn't. I mean, when we got your call to come immediately, we did."

"So you didn't talk to them?"

"No, sir."

Morgan sighed. "Well, that's one thing we'll need to do."

Grave spoke up. "How do you want to proceed, captain? Shall we bring in the SanniClaws for questioning?"

Morgan considered the idea, but only briefly. "No, no Grave. First, I'd like to get the results from this machine. How did Superman die and are there any clues in the method of death that will lead us to his killer? Polk, how long will this process take?"

Polk studied the gauges on the control panel. "The estimated time to completion is four hours, forty-seven minutes."

Morgan raised his eyebrows. "Not exactly the speediest machine, is it?"

Polk was happy to accept any criticism of the ME-4350. "No, not speedy at all. On the other hand, it is said, this machine is 99.7 percent accurate in its readings, so perhaps the wait will be worth it."

Morgan looked around the room and considered his options. They could all sit there and wait, but Morgan didn't like the idea of having his team idle for nearly half a day. No, he'd send the teams off in different directions to gather further evidence. The only question was where to send each. They all had different skillsets and approached crime scenes in different ways.

In Captain Morgan's experience, there were at least four kinds of detectives when it came to evidence. The first kind would look at a leaf-strewn crime scene, note each leaf and its placement, and look for patterns. The second kind would rake the leaves, or clues, into a pile, hoping that the preponderance of evidence would point to the criminal. The third kind, whom Morgan called berserkers, would kick through the leaf pile, hoping that the disturbance would flush the criminal from hiding. The fourth kind, who exhibited extreme patience, would wait for the right leaves to blow their way. For this last kind, the crime seemed to solve itself as the detective watched patiently.

And in truth, Morgan recognized that every detective was a unique blend of all four kinds, with one kind dominant. Charlize and Smithers were first-kind dominant; Loblolly second-kind; Snoot third-kind; and Grave and Blunt fourth-kind. Morgan himself was a unique fifth kind, whose hallmark was impatience, making him eminently suitable as a captain—he wanted results, *now*.

"All right," he said, "here's what we'll do."

After each detective had briefed the others on what they had found and not found at the various hovercycle clubs—which was precious little—Morgan reconfigured the detective teams back into their usual, everyday teams: Grave with Blunt, Charlize with Smithers, and Snoot with Loblolly, and sent them off to do additional follow-up investigations.

Grave and Blunt were sent to the Sons, Snoot and Loblolly to the Vie Kings, and Charlize and Smithers to the Krypto Knights. Morgan saved the SanniClaws for himself. He was on friendly terms with them, and if they really were the killers, he might be just the man to trip them up.

21

Charlize and Smithers didn't even have to knock on the door of the Krypto Knight's clubhouse. The sound of the approaching Duesenberg had alerted the club, and they had all poured out of the building to watch its approach and gather around the vehicle as it came to a stop.

"That's quite a vehicle," said one as Charlize and Smithers stepped out.

"Indeed," said Charlize. "A 1929 Duesenberg, or at least a reasonable replica."

The man whistled through his teeth. "It looks like it's moving standing still."

"The effect of great design," said Smithers.

The man nodded back, then squinted at them, getting down to business. "You were here several hours ago. May I ask why?"

Charlize was never one to sugarcoat bad news. "Yes, I'm afraid I must report that your president, Chase Arnold, has been murdered."

The man took a step back, shocked, as did the other club members. "Superman? How? When? What? I don't understand."

"We're still looking into each of those questions," said Smithers. "Which is why we're here."

"Indeed," said Charlize. "May we go inside? We'd like to ask you a few questions."

The man nodded, motioned to the other club members, and began moving to the door. "This way."

Charlize and Smithers followed them in, not at all expecting to see what the outside of the building suggested they would see. No paintings of monsters, no museum cases filled with dubious evidence of cryptid existence—nothing like that at all.

What they found was a high-tech, open concept office floor filled with computers surrounded by multiple floor-to-ceiling screens, each filled with tables, charts, and flowing data.

The man noticed their surprise. "Everyone reacts this way at first. They think we're cryptozoology kooks, and while all that is very true, we make our living in the area of cybersecurity."

"Hacking?" said Charlize.

The man laughed. "Well, yes and no. We're more the guys who track the hackers and protect the data owners."

"Very impressive," said Smithers. "But why is it that we are just learning this?"

"Pardon?" said the man.

"I think he means," said Charlize, "why has an operation like this gone undetected by the Crab Cove Police?"

The man shrugged. "This is the first time the police have actually set foot on our premises. You've been here before, of course, outside at least, but the cryptid paintings kept you from prying further. You think, or thought, we were hovercycle kooks."

Charlize nodded. "As Smithers said, this is all very impressive, and I'd like to discuss your operation further, but first there are more pressing matters."

"Superman," said the man.

"Yes," said Charlize. She stretched out her hand. "I'm Detective Charlize Holmes and this is my assistant, Doctor Smithers-Watson."

The man nodded and took her hand. "Larry Abrams, the vice president. Everyone calls me Kent."

Charlize suppressed a laugh. He was the very image of Superman's alter ego, Clark Kent, from the suit to the glasses to his square-jawed good looks. She could easily imagine him running into a phone booth, ripping off his clothes, and emerging as Superman. "After *Clark* Kent, I presume."

"The very one," he said. "Now, if you'll join us at our council table, we'll answer your questions."

Charlize and Smithers moved to the table and sat down, each of the club members finding seats opposite them, with Kent in the middle. He was their president now, and the realization seemed to be taking effect on him. He was the new Superman.

"Well," said Charlize. "Let's start with some basic information, shall we?"

Kent nodded. "Anything."

"Very well," said Charlize, turning to Smithers. "Please record, audio and video."

Smithers nodded and sat back in his seat, knowing he'd have no chance to speak now. Charlize was in control, and he was perfectly fine with that.

"So," said Charlize, turning back to Kent. "When was the last time you saw him?"

Question followed question, Kent responding, the others nodding their heads in agreement. The last anyone had seen Superman was the previous evening. Everything seemed to be fine, then at about nine, he'd received a call, and without talking to anyone, he'd raced from the building and sped away on his hovercycle, followed by his drone, Olsen. Neither Kent nor the others knew any reason for his alarm or actions. The club was into nothing criminal or nefarious, at least according to Kent. They were just a cybersecurity firm, doing what they do best.

Charlize and Smithers thanked them for their time, climbed back into the Duesenberg, and sped away, the two riding in silence for some time.

"Something's not right," said Charlize, finally.

"Agreed," said Smithers. "They know more than they're saying."

"Indeed, and it shall all be revealed if I have any say in the matter."

Smithers nodded. "What now?"

"The captain said to reassemble at the station once we'd completed our preliminary interviews, so it's back to the squad room, I guess."

They rode along in silence, then Smithers suddenly perked up. "Charlize."

"Yes?"

"Did you notice the number of drones?"

"What?"

"If my count is right, there were ten more than the number of club members."

Sometimes Smithers surprised her. She hadn't noticed the discrepancy at all. "Excellent, Smithers. What do you make of it?"

"Well, they could be delivery drones."

Charlize considered the possibility. "But they have no physical product to deliver."

"True enough. What about messenger drones?"

"Messenger drones? To whom and for what purpose? They have all the computer power they need to send encrypted messages to anyone, anywhere."

Smithers realized there was only one alternative left, but he was incredulous at the possibility. "*Burner* drones?"

Charlize nodded agreement. "Yes, but that's just as mysterious. Why would they need burner drones?"

"I don't know. Perhaps they're building them and selling them."

Charlize pondered the possibility. "All is not as it seems, Smithers. Let's think on this. Perhaps the other teams' efforts will help us fill in the gaps in our understanding."

"Yes," said Smithers, "yes." It was clear from his tone and the way he had dragged out the second *yes* that he had more to say.

"What?" said Charlize.

"Um, well, there's one more thing that's been nagging me."

"Oh?"

"Where is Superman's hovercycle—and his drone, Olsen?"

"Indeed," she said. "Indeed."

There was also something that was nagging at Charlize. "What do you make of that seagull, Smithers?"

Smithers was taken aback. He was already wrestling with the possible location of Superman's hovercycle and Olsen. "What? What do you mean?"

"You know, just your general impression."

Smithers sighed. "Well, he's a curiosity, I'll give him that. And I suppose the technology itself is a marvel." He shrugged, trying to contribute more, but failed. "I don't know. What do you make of him?"

"I'm not sure, but every time I look at him, I get the feeling that I should know more, that he holds a clue to *something*, I don't know what."

"Shall we have a chat with him, then?"

Charlize nodded slowly, already formulating her questions. "Yes, good idea." She slapped both hands on her knees. "All right, let's head on back to the station, but by way of the boardwalk."

"Boardwalk?"

"Yes, we'll need some boardwalk fries."

The Duesenberg picked up speed, the simulated sound of its engine growing louder. It was almost like a growl.

22

As Detectives Snoot and Loblolly drove to the clubhouse of the Vie Kings, Loblolly kept glancing over at Snoot.

"What?" said Snoot finally.

Loblolly chuckled. "Nothing."

"No, come on, what's that Cheshire grin about?"

Loblolly laughed louder. "It's just good to see the driver of this hovercruiser, is all."

Snoot gave her a questioning look, then realized what she meant, and laughed. "You mean Blunt?"

Loblolly nodded. "It near scared me to death. I could barely see the man."

Snoot chuckled. "Yeah, it's an acquired skill all right. It took me months to figure out where he was in a room. Even now, I sometimes get it wrong."

"He seems a good man, though. And I like his wife as well, although she's as much a challenge to see."

"She is, though not as hard to see as her daughter, Rippley."

Loblolly shook her head. "You got that right. That little girl is a wonder."

"And a pistol."

"She is that." Loblolly looked ahead. They were just a mile or so from the turnoff to the Vie Kings. "So, what do we know about the Vie Kings?"

Snoot cleared her throat. "Well, precious little from Charlize's visit. She was redirected, remember?"

"Yes, but what then? Are we going in blind?"

Snoot chuckled. "Oh, no. I'm familiar with them. As crazy as they seem—wait till you get a load of the clubhouse and their members—they're heavy into the spice trade."

"Really? Then why haven't they been shut down?"

"A good question. They've certainly been under surveillance long enough. But they're sneaky good at what they do."

"But if they're dealing in spice, how could they even cover the smell. I mean Old Bay is pretty strong, as is New Bay."

"Yes, good point, and one of the mysteries with these guys. The feeling is they have a secret laboratory somewhere, where they can openly work with the spice without fear of the smell betraying them."

"Perhaps on one of their crab boats, the ones that look like Viking ships."

"Maybe, or perhaps in a cave."

The word *cave* startled Loblolly. "You mean like the cave where Chester Clink was hiding?"

Snoot nodded. Just days ago, they had pursued the elusive serial killer through the cave system below the home of Lachlan McLachlan, the inventor who had been murdered during the Orville Murder Case. "Could be, but a different cave, surely."

"Yes, we would have noticed the smell."

"Right," said Snoot, pointing ahead. "Look, here's our turn."

"Okay, great. Anyway, so are the Vie Kings just supplying the spice or are they cutting it and adding the whatsit, that drug?"

Snoot frowned. "We're not sure, at least not yet. The whatsit, the drug you're thinking of, is Vitol, a hallucinogen straight from Mars. Together they make up what the street kids call Steamers or Reds or Martians when it's cut with Old Bay, and Blue Claw or Blues or Big Blue Marbles when it's cut with New Bay."

"Yeah, I know, and White Martians when it's straight Vitol."

Snoot chuckled sardonically. "Yeah, the good old red, white, and blue." She pointed through the window again. "Here we are."

The Quonset longhouse-clubhouse of the Vie Kings loomed in front of them, and in front of the clubhouse a tall man loomed over a smaller man. Each wore a horned helmet, as did the tiny drones hovering over their heads.

"The tall one is Harold "Bluetooth" Mortenson, their president," said Snoot.

Loblolly nodded "So the little red-headed guy must be Filip "Pokie" Sigurdsen, right?"

"Yes, he's the vice president and what they call their *Hofgothi*, kind of like a priest or a medicine man. Into magic and occult Viking shit."

Loblolly chuckled. "Well, this should be fun. Shall we get out?"

"That's why we're here, Polly. Okay, detective faces on."

They stepped out of the hovercruiser, each with take-no-prisoners frowns that made Bluetooth and Pokie take a step back.

Snoot took the lead, striding up to them and coming to a hands-on-hips stop right under the nose of Bluetooth. She stared right up his nostrils. "You must be Bluetooth," she said.

Bluetooth nodded and turned to Pokie. "Yeah, and this is Pokie."

Snoot kept her eyes fixed on Bluetooth's nostrils. "I know that." She turned and nodded at Loblolly, who had taken up a similar stance directly behind Snoot. "And this here is Detective Loblolly."

Loblolly pointed to Pine Cone, who was hovering at her shoulder. "And this is my drone, Pine Cone."

Bluetooth looked back at Snoot. "You have no drone?"

"It's a long, sad story," she said. "Let's just say I'm between drones."

"Ah," said Bluetooth, pointing at his drone. "This is Odin."

Pokie chimed in. "And this is Loki, after the god of the same name."

"Yes, of course," said Loblolly. "The trickster, the shape-shifter, son of Fárbauti and Laufey, and the brother of Helblindi and Býleistr."

Pokie's eyes grew wide. "You know your Norse."

Loblolly shrugged. "Part Norwegian on my father's side. He told me tales."

Pokie looked at her expectantly, as if he were hoping she would begin a tale for him. "I would hear more. Won't you come inside? We have laid out a modest feast."

"You were expecting us?" said Snoot.

"No," said Bluetooth. "We do this every day. Our men will return from their crab boats soon, and their hunger will be fierce."

"We have many questions," said Snoot.

"And we have an equal number of answers, perhaps more," said Bluetooth. He stepped aside and beckoned them to follow him through the front door of the longhouse.

Snoot nodded at Loblolly, and the two of them followed Bluetooth and Pokie into the longhouse, Pine Cone and the other drones following.

Pokie directed them to a bench at their long table, he and Bluetooth sitting down opposite them, a smorgasbord of food between them: herring and crab and all manner of delicacies.

"Eat," said Bluetooth.

Snoot smiled at him. "We shall, but first a few questions if you don't mind."

"By all means," he said.

"Yes," said Pokie, laughing. "But as Odin always said, *listen carefully before you judge a man.*"

"Fair enough," said Snoot as Loblolly chuckled beside her. "What?"

Loblolly directed her gaze at Pokie. "I believe you left off the next line from the Hávámál: *Don't ever mock or laugh at a guest or wayfarer.*"

Pokie squinted at her, then waved his hand over the food. "He also said *the night is friendly when the food is plenty.*"

Loblolly cocked her head, not ready to be outdone. "Followed by *scoff not at the guest, nor drive him to the door; be kind to beggars.*"

Bluetooth slammed his fist on the table, silencing them both. "More important, Pokie, and as you well know, Odin always said *it's good manners to give your guest conversation and a chance to speak.*"

Pokie frowned and looked down at the table. "He also said *a man may sit at the feast in friendly conversation before he learns he has dined with foes.*"

Bluetooth slammed his fist on the table again. "Silence!"

Pokie nodded, crossed his arms, and looked at the ceiling.

Satisfied that Pokie would remain quiet, Bluetooth turned back to Snoot with a smile. "Your questions then."

23

He was shaking his head, or appeared to be shaking his head, a nuanced motion that Grave had only recently been able to detect coming from an otherwise cloudlike form known as Sergeant Barry Blunt.

"What?" said Grave.

"Nothing," said Blunt, the head-like part of the cloud-man continuing to shake. "It's just that I don't see the point."

"The point?"

"In going back to the clubhouses so soon. Wouldn't it be better to just wait until cause and manner of death—not to mention location of death—was known before following up."

To Grave's mind, Blunt had a point, but he could also understand Captain Morgan's eagerness to get more information. "The thing is, we were only at the Sons for twenty minutes or so. We were looking for a body at that point, and the phone calls kept pointing us in new directions. This will really be our first chance to talk to the Sons in depth."

The cloud-man sighed. "I get that, but it would still be good to have a better understanding of Superman's death. It would certainly help us frame our questions."

"I see your point, I do, but at this point, I think we have to take Superman's own words into account. He said we would find his body at the Sons' clubhouse. Presumably, the Sons or one of the Sons, had something to do with his death."

"Yes, that's possible, but a lot of things are possible. I mean, calling in the whereabouts of your body certainly calls into question your motives."

"So you think he was trying to place blame where it doesn't belong."

"Sir, I've heard of premeditated murder, but never premeditated victimhood. Something stinks about this."

Grave laughed. "*Premeditated victimhood,* huh. I like that. And it tells me just where we need to start our line of questioning."

"Sir?"

"Motives, Blunt, and relationships. How are Superman and the Krypto Knights tied to the Sons? Is there bad blood between them? Any recent events that shed light on the situation?"

"I see what you mean, sir. That does make some sense."

The hovercruiser slowed to a stop in front of the Sons clubhouse.

"Look," said Grave. "There's a lot of people to talk to here. Let's divide and conquer. I'll take the club officers and you take the other men."

"What about their old ladies?"

"Them, too, if you have the chance. Start with the where-were-you-on-the-night-of question and go from there."

"Sounds good."

"Okay, and let's send Object and Barry off to explore, see if they notice anything unusual around here while we conduct our interviews."

Grave and Blunt climbed out of the police hovercruiser, whispered instructions to Barry and Object, and headed for the front door of the clubhouse.

A young man and an older woman were standing by the door, arms crossed, waiting for them.

A mother and her son, thought Grave. *Must be Pax and his mother, Sookie.*

24

Captain Henry Morgan had known Bruce "Brush" Langley, president of the SanniClaws, his entire career. In fact, the two of them had started their lives in civil service on the same day some forty-five years ago. They'd even attended the same orientation seminar, sitting next to each other as a droning city official explained the whats, whens, and wherefores of life in the service of Crab Cove.

As the years went by, their paths crossed on many occasions, usually during storm cleanup following hurricanes or more often in less dramatic events, when the rising waters of the Atlantic took another building along the shores of Crab Cove.

They often joked that their jobs were similar. Both, they reasoned, were trying to clean up the town, just in different ways, involving different connotations of *trash* and *garbage.*

So when Captain Morgan rolled up in his police hovercruiser, Brush was not the least bit worried. If anything, he was glad to see his old friend.

"How's it hangin', Hank?" said Brush.

Morgan chuckled. Brush was among the few he allowed to call him that. "Loosey-goosey and low. How's the trash business?"

"Ever growing, cap'n, ever growing."

"Just like crime, or so it seems."

Brush nodded. "I blame the Mars Terminal. Bringing in too many outsiders, and the ones returning are all messed up in the head, if you ask me."

Morgan, if pressed, would have had to agree. The people heading to Mars thought they could get away with little crimes before they departed Earth, and the people returning were traumatized, many strung out on drugs, willing to do anything for a Red, White, or Blue. "I hear you."

Brush tugged up his pants, a sign that Morgan well knew meant that the topic of conversation was about to change. "So, I hear you're looking for a body. That why you're here?"

"And how would you know that?"

Brush laughed. "Crab Cove is not exactly a big city, Hank. Word on the street, or at least the parade route, is that Superman is dead."

Morgan nodded. "Oh, he is that, but he just keeps moving around town. We even heard he was right here at your doorstep."

"Here?"

"Yeah, we received a call."

Brush scratched his head, perhaps far beyond feigned puzzlement required. "You don't say."

"Yep, said we'd find the body right here."

"Well, if that don't beat all. Why would Superman's body end up here?"

Morgan cocked his head. "Brush, you know that's why I'm here, so let's cut to the chase. Was the body here?"

Brush sighed. "Dammit, Hank, you know I can't lie to you. Yes, yes, the body was here."

"And you didn't think to call me."

"Hank, Hank, I was going to, but then the rest of the fellas thought we should just put the body where you'd easily find it."

Morgan grunted. "Yeah, at the morgue, after thoroughly washing the body and putting it into a forensics pod."

Brush looked surprised. "Um, no, *hell no,* we dropped it in front of City Hall. You know how I hate the mayor. Thought it would be a good way to embarrass that bitch."

Something about his reply suggested there was more to tell, but Captain Morgan was too busy trying to close his own mouth, which had dropped open, words failing. *Who in hell moved the body to the morgue?*

25

Sally "Sookie" Banks Edwards, mother of Patrick "Pax" Banks and wife of Clarence "Claw" Edwards, was a highly accomplished practitioner of the icy stare. She was approaching fifty, but dressed like she was eighteen, even though tight jeans and a halter top no longer showed off the tight butt and perky breasts she'd once had, now victims of gravity. But she was still a handsome woman, even sexy, icy stare and all.

"What the hell do you guys want now? Like we told you, there's no missing body here."

Detective Grave smiled back at her icy stare, with little effect. "We know that."

"Then what the hell?" said Pax, moving between his mother and Grave. "Get out of here."

Even on his best days, Grave was an *almost* handsome man. But this man, this man was the epitome of handsome. Tall and well-built, his every feature—eyes, nose, lips, hair, teeth—seemed to be conspiring with one another to create a man that made women gasp at the first sight of him. There was a swagger to him. But perhaps not enough swagger to deal with a near invisible man.

The cloud that was Sergeant Barry Blunt grabbed Pax by the arm and tugged him away from Grave, almost lifting him off his feet, leaving him wide-eyed, swagger free, and confused.

"What the—" said Pax, breaking Blunt's hold. He turned back to Grave. "What, you have invisible detectives now?"

Grave smiled at him. "We do, so you better watch out. They're everywhere."

Sookie sighed. "Seriously, detective whatever-your-name-is . . ."

"Grave. Detective Simon Grave."

She chuckled. "Shit, the guy with that old Austin Healey Sprite with the radio cranked up with gospel music?"

Grave nodded. "The very same."

"You're the one who should be arrested, for disturbing the peace."

Grave smiled back at her indulgently. "I'm not here to arrest anyone."

"No?" said Pax. "Then piss off."

Grave shook his head. "Come on, you know I can get a warrant and be back here in two seconds with twenty simdroid officers ready to tear your clubhouse apart. All I want is a little conversation. Answers to a few questions."

Sookie frowned and put her hands on her hips, defiant. "Look, there's no body here. Never been a body here. We told you that."

"And how do you even know it was Superman?" said Pax.

Grave shrugged. "It was definitely Superman, and yes, we know there's no body here."

"Then what the—" Pax began.

Grave held up a hand, stopping him. "We *do* know that there's nobody here, but we *also know* that in the last few hours the body has had a whirlwind tour of every hovercycle clubhouse in Crab Cove."

Pax and Sookie blinked in a way that suggested to Grave that they had just received new information. Grave had no doubt that the chain of events had begun here, at the clubhouse of The Sons of Irony, just as Superman had told them.

The Sons had moved the body, no doubt about that either. The question was whether they were covering up a crime or just trying to get themselves out of an unexpected situation, namely a body self-delivered to their door through no fault of their own.

Grave looked back and forth at them. "Now, can we have our little talk?"

26

Doctor Smithers-Watson, set to record, could not help enjoying the conversation between Charlize and the curiosity that was the talking seagull, Horace. Charlize was on her game, as was this remarkable bird. The good doctor's databanks suggested various analogies, but Smithers-Watson thought a championship tennis match was most apt, each player testing the other, each player at the very limits of their game.

"Have we met before?" said Charlize, probing.

Horace tried his best to speak, but his answer was garbled by a beak and mouth crammed with cold French fries.

"What was that?" said Charlize.

"Mmph," said Horace by way of explanation.

"Swallow, then talk," said Charlize. She glanced over at Smithers-Watson. "You're recording this, right?"

"Yes, of course. Audio and video."

"Good." She turned back to Horace, who had managed to take a break from his rapacious attack on a supersized funnel of fries. "I said, not to my knowledge."

"But you were McLachlan's bird, right?"

"Well, *he* thought so, but I assure you I've always been quite independent." He eyed the French fries.

Seeing what was about to come next, Charlize moved the fries out of reach.

"Hey," said Horace. "No fair."

"You'll get them back as soon as we're done here."

Horace shook his head. "You simdroids are as bad as humans. Always want your way. And here I am, a poor, hungry bird denied sustenance."

"Just answer a few questions, and the fries will be yours. Perhaps I'll even send a drone out for more."

Horace perked up. "Now you're talking. Let's get on with it. Yes, I was McLachlan's bird, although experimental flying rat was the regard he held me in. I was no pet, that's for sure."

"Yes, I understand that. He was testing a neural node, which given your eloquence and intelligence, was successful."

"Indeed," said Horace, puffing up his feathers. "I'm a marvel, no doubt about that. But seriously, what more can I tell you? He lured us with French fries, took us back to his laboratory, and performed the necessary surgeries."

Charlize's eyes blinked rapidly. "What do you mean, *us?*"

Horace shrugged his wings. "Why, Arnold and me."

"Arnold?"

"Yeah, my best bud."

The importance of what he was saying slowly dawned on Charlize. When she had investigated the crime scene at McLachlan's house and laboratory, she remembered there were two empty cages.

"Two of you? So where is this Arnold now?"

Horace shrugged again. "No idea."

"But didn't he help you with the attack on the drones?"

Horace shook his head. "Nope. Say, can I have at least one French fry?"

Charlize sighed. "Yes, I suppose." She tossed him a French fry, which he caught and gobbled down. "So, so . . ."

"So he's elsewhere, probably still in the clutches of the man we thought was setting us free. I escaped, as you can see, but Arnold was not so lucky."

"Man?"

"Yes, yes, a man. We'd seen him before, while we were still locked in our cages. He'd peek in the windows, and we'd scream for help."

Charlize was beginning to fully grasp what the bird was saying, although it was almost unbelievable. "By any chance was this a man of medium build with a blondish gray crewcut?"

Horace perked up. "Why, yes."

"And pale blue eyes?"

"Yes, freaky pale, like the sky in winter. No, paler than that."

And now it all rushed back to her. They had pursued Clink through the cave system under McLachlan's house, but weren't able to prevent his escape by submarine. Charlize remembered picking up a seagull feather at the underground dock.

"Chester Clink," she said, finally. "Serial killer extraordinaire."

Horace squawked. "Serial killer? Holy fish heads."

"Not to worry," said Charlize. "He only kills people, usually young women."

"Oh," said Horace. "Say, can I have those French fries now?"

27

Over the years, as his experience as a detective grew, Detective Grave found that he much preferred in-depth interviews with single subjects rather than group interviews, which tended to provide only cursory information while opening up the real possibility of unnecessary tangential conversations. His way of thinking, right or wrong, was that he would get more from less and less from more when it came to the number of people being interviewed.

So he would have more or less preferred to start with Claw and work his way down the chain of command from Claw to Pax to Fiddler and then the others. That would have given him the opportunity to know more, and through separate conversations, verify information and alibis. On the other hand, since it was not clear that the Sons were involved in a murder—this whole affair could have been Superman's idea of a vengeful suicide—he opted for a group meeting as a reasonable way to begin. Additional interviews could then follow, more or less.

After a brief aside with Sergeant Blunt, he decided to interview them all at once, with Blunt at his side, free to jump in whenever he felt the need. And so it was that they now sat around the club's long table, Grave and Blunt at one end with Barry and Object hovering at their shoulders, and Claw at the other end, surrounded by the other Sons according to their rank within the club.

Claw took a few minutes to introduce each.

Oakley "Oakie" Kent was at the top of the list. He was the oldest member, and with age, had become cantankerous and unruly, striking out against even the slightest offense. Like Claw, his cuts featured a Men of Ahem patch, which recognized an act of sublime irony in a time of stress, as well as a Bloody 9 patch, a someone ironic patch recognizing that he had bloodied himself by falling off his hovercycle nine times. Also like Claw, he was tall and barrel chested, but that's where the similarities ended. Oakie had a beer gut big as a keg, his head was too small for his body, and his eyes were too large for his head, making him appear to be a caricature of a person and not a living man. His personal drone, Piney, hovered near his shoulder.

Manny "Andy" Kent, Oakie's son and best friend to Claw's son, Pax, was blessed with his father's size and his mother's features. It was as if the father's grotesque features had been smoothed and reshaped by a talented sculptor, the result a handsome young man with piercing blue eyes and a smile that could light up rooms. A fairly new member, his cuts had but one patch, the Sons of Irony back patch, a silver shield with a whimsical steamed crab upon an American flag, an eagle hovering above him, ready to strike. His drone was named Opie.

James "Jerry Lee" Lewis, who supplemented his Sons of Irony take on profits with gigs impersonating rock singer Jerry Lee Lewis, complete with piano banging, was the club's Mallet Master, as his mallet patch clearly indicated. In addition to performing sergeant-at-arms duties, he also organized the club's periodic crab feasts. Of all the members, he was the smallest and the roundest. He looked like a large ball on legs, and no one would ever describe him as handsome. If anything, he seemed to be more related to a pug than a human. His drone was Elvis.

Charles "Crabs" Morris, known for being on the giving and receiving end of knives, had a scar that ran from his right ear to the corner of his mouth, where it ended in a thin-lipped sneer, the man's favorite expression. He had eyes and a nose, of course, but all you ever noticed was his scar, and he took offense if you stared too long at it. He was a measured man, in the way he spoke and the way he moved, every word and move considered and intentional. A Man of Ahem of the first order, Crabs was proud of his single patch. He definitely wasn't seeking a Bloody 9 patch; he just didn't appreciate the irony of a patch extolling failure. His drone, Chibs, bobbed up and down above his head.

Bruce "Fid" Norman, like Andy, only had the club patch on his cuts. But that was fine with Fid. Glory and recognition were two things he never sought. He wanted to blend into the crowd and, most of all, not be an asshole. Still, there was one way he stood out: he couldn't speak without gesturing with his hands. That's why they called him Fid; he just seemed to be fiddling with his hands nonstop. Of all the members of the Sons of Irony, he seemed out of place. Take off his cuts and you'd swear you were looking at a nondescript nine-to-fiver, an accountant perhaps or an insurance salesman. His drone was Tig.

Pablo "Smoothie" Cruz, the only Latino in the club, was as bald as a cue ball, with red lightning bolt tattoos on either side of his head, making him look like some kind of superhero, albeit in a short, small frame. Smoothie was on the cusp of being patched in and was still trying to make the transition from go-fer to full member, an effort that required leaving obsequiousness behind in favor of attitude and swagger, a trait his drone, Juice, also exhibited.

As each person and their drones were introduced, Grave acknowledged them with a polite nod, occasionally glancing at his watch to let Claw know that he needn't go into detail about each member. Sergeant Blunt, on the other hand, seemed to be stifling a laugh throughout the course of the introductions, which clearly got on Claw's nerves.

Claw was about to introduce his wife, Sookie, and his son, Pax, but Blunt's chuckle set him off. "What's with your barely visible friend? He seems to find us amusing."

Blunt shook his head, not that he was sure anyone could see his head moving. For most, he was just a swirling cloud that formed into a man from time to time. "Sorry, I meant no offense. It's just that your drones seem to be named after characters in an old television show from the beginning of the century, the Sons of Anarchy." He looked over at Sookie and Pax. "I bet your drones are called Gemma and Jax. Am I right?"

Claw nodded. "Yes, very perceptive of you, sergeant. As it turns out, we use various episodes from that show to train our prospects. They can't patch in until they pass a rigorous series of examinations based on those episodes."

"So you're fans of the Sons of Anarchy." Grave meant it as a statement, but Claw took it as a silly question.

"Not at all. We use the episodes to show our prospects how *not* to behave and how *not* to go about our business. We're honest tradesmen who like to ride hovercycles, and that's it. We're certainly not low-life criminals like the Sons of Anarchy."

"But you named your drones after those characters," said Blunt. "Why?"

Claw cocked his head and smiled. "Just a bit of irony, is all."

"Wait," said Grave. "Why didn't you use those nicknames for yourselves?"

Claw laughed. "How silly would that have been? No, we choose our own nicknames, which makes it doubly ironic." He lifted his arms for all to see and gave Grave an icy stare. "Like my tattoos here, detective. Trouble and Trouble, for double trouble. And me such a peaceful man. No trouble at all."

"More irony," said Grave.

"Indeed," said Claw. "Indeed."

28

One of the good things about owning a personal drone was that you could always have a heart-to-motherboard talk without anyone questioning your sanity. So it was with Captain Morgan and his drone, Rum, an older model drone that Morgan had dressed up to look like the real-deal Captain Henry Morgan of rum label fame. A little additional programming and Rum could wield the two little cutlasses that Morgan had made for him in his garage cum metal shop. Still more programming and Rum could use the cutlasses for a variety of nuanced emotions.

So as the police hovercruiser headed back to the station on autopilot, Morgan turned to Rum to get his take on what had transpired at the SanniClaws clubhouse, particularly Brush's admission of moving the body.

Rum swung a cutlass above his rotors. "It was a crime, sir. A clear criminal act. Why didn't you arrest him on the spot?"

Morgan knew he should have, so his sigh had a guilty edge to it. "You're right, of course, but I wanted to get input from my teams before proceeding further."

Rum jabbed his cutlass into the air, clearly upset. "Input? Who the hell's in charge here, you or them?"

Morgan shook his head. He wasn't sure anymore. As he approached retirement he questioned himself more and more every day. Should they do this, should they do that, should they do anything at all? He was losing the confidence required of a leader of men, women, simdroids, and drones, and he knew it. "You're right, of course, *they are.*"

Rum, exasperated, threw his swords onto the seat next to Morgan. "What? What did you say? I can't believe my audio input."

Morgan nodded. "Yes, yes, I know I should take charge, but well, hell, I should just retire, don't you think? Find a little umbrella on the beach and just soak in the sun."

Now Rum was really angry. "What, so I can fight off seagulls all day? Not on your life, cap'n."

"No, Rum, I'm getting too old for this job. Time to let someone younger take over."

"And who in hell would that be, sir?"

Morgan tried to think who would be the best fit for the job, but every name that popped up had him shaking his head with increasing force. "Well, you have a point."

"Exactly, sir. They'd have to bring someone in from outside, someone with zero knowledge of your teams, maybe even of Crab Cove. Why, sir, it would set the force back years. Crime would be out of control before you knew it."

"You think?"

"Sir, I know. Why, it wouldn't even be safe to sit on our beaches. We'd have to move inland, find a cabin in the mountains."

Morgan shook his head. "I don't like mountains."

"Nor I, sir. So promise me you'll stay on the job."

Morgan wasn't so sure. "But Rum, I'm too old for this shit."

"Shit, sir, *shit?* Why you're the only man in this town who has his shit together enough to keep Crab Cove safe from the criminal elements that swirl around it."

"You really think that?"

"I do, sir, I do. There's not a single other person capable enough to replace you."

"What about Charlize? She's programmed with the skills of every known detective."

"Compared to you, sir, she's just a bucket of logic. You, sir, have *instincts.*"

Morgan had to admit that Rum was onto something. Yes, by god, he did have instincts, instincts that had pointed many an investigation in the right direction toward a swift and satisfyingly accurate conclusion. This realization puffed Morgan up a bit. "I do, don't I?"

"Indeed, sir, indeed you do."

"Why, I could do this a little longer, surely."

Rum was delighted enough to retrieve his cutlasses and jab one at the roof of the hovercruiser. "You could do this, sir, *forever*."

Morgan chuckled. "Well, let's not get too far ahead of ourselves, Rum. Let's get through this case and then think about the future."

"Excellent, sir. Now, what are your instincts telling you about this case? What should we do next?"

Morgan sat back in his seat, his arms folded across his chest, his eyes staring at the roof of the hovercruiser, a posture that Rum instantly recognized: the cap'n was thinking, thinking hard.

"Don't think too hard, cap'n. Use those instincts of yours, sir."

Morgan came out of his trance and smiled broadly at Rum. "What we're going to do is follow a lead, Rum."

"A lead, sir? What lead?"

"Don't you see, Rum? The SanniClaws say they dumped the body in front of City Hall. If that's true, and I have no reason to doubt what Brush told me, then someone at City Hall may have been the person who dropped off the body at the morgue."

Rum waved both swords over his rotors. "Why, sir, I think you're onto something."

Morgan puffed up. "Indeed, I am, Rum. Now, let's get this damned hovercruiser headed in the right direction."

He began punching buttons on the console. "City Hall here we come!"

29

Detective Amanda Snoot and Detective Polly Loblolly had been partners for only a few weeks and were still trying to figure each other out. Snoot had already learned that Loblolly was a nervous passenger and preferred to drive whenever possible. She had also learned that Loblolly drove like a lead-footed maniac, which made Snoot, an otherwise unflappable person, the nervous passenger.

"Slow down," she said as calmly as she could while stomping on her invisible passenger-side brakes.

Loblolly eased off the accelerator, and the hovercruiser dutifully slowed.

Snoot puffed out her cheeks and sighed in relief. "Boy, the way you drive."

Loblolly chuckled. "Sorry, I just like to get from Point A to Point B."

"They may as well be one point the way you drive."

Loblolly sighed. "All right, then, looks like with this pokey driving, we'll have some time to discuss the case. What do you think?"

Snoot contemplated the question. Bluetooth and Pokie had been less than forthcoming, and the questions had been cut short when the rest of the Vie Kings came charging in and attacked the smorgasbord. "Well, I'd say they're guilty of something, but probably not the murder."

"Yeah, for sure. Did you notice the way they both blinked every time we mentioned Superman?"

"Yes, I'm sure the body was there, and I'm sure they moved it, but *why* the body was there and *why* they moved it is still a mystery."

Loblolly nodded. "Yeah, maybe one of the other teams will be able to shed some light on that."

"I wonder," said Snoot.

"Wonder? About what?"

"These clubs. They hate each other, but interact with one another in certain areas."

"Their *businesses*."

"Yeah, but also their nefarious dealings. We need to map those out, see where the stress points might be."

"Sounds like a plan," said Loblolly, "but dollars to donuts, the biggest stress point is between Superman and the Sons. I mean, why would he tell us his body would be found at their clubhouse?"

"Yeah, we keep coming back to that, but the sequence of events, the way the body was moved from one clubhouse to the next, could reveal additional stressors. What did Superman have against the Sons, yes? But also, why did the Sons move the body to the Vie Kings, why did the Vie Kings move the body to the SanniClaws?"

"And why did *they* move it to the morgue?"

Snoot sighed. "Yeah, yeah, and how do the Krypto Knights fit in this puzzle? Hell, the whole damned thing makes me hungry."

Loblolly gave Snoot a look of disbelief. "Hungry? After that smorgasbord?"

Snoot laughed. "I may be thin and wiry, but I have an appetite that's pretty much unmatched."

"Jeez, I wish I had your metabolism. I get fat if I so much as look at food."

"Tell you what," said Snoot. "Take the next turn."

"Why? That'll take us through town. We'll be late to the station."

"No, seriously, it will be all right. Just take a few minutes or so, and besides, it will give me a chance to point out some of the city landmarks and tourist traps."

Loblolly had learned by now that resistance was futile when Snoot set her mind on something. She was a real bulldog in that regard. Sometimes, it was a fault, but sometimes it was a real asset, particularly in investigations. "All right, all right, have your way. Here's the turn. So where to first?"

Snoot gave her a devious smile. "You'll see. Just wait till we make the turn. Our destination will become apparent soon enough."

Loblolly made the turn and slowed the hovercruiser, not knowing for sure how far they would be going from here. "Okay, what now?"

Snoot chuckled. "You'll see. Wait for it, wait for it."

And then Loblolly threw her head back and laughed. "Oh, no, you can't mean it."

"Oh, yeah," said Snoot. "Behold, the Skunk 'n Donuts, maker of donuts par excellence."

30

Grave sat in silence as Sergeant Blunt practiced the evil art of driving while invisible. The meeting with the Sons had gone about as expected. They saw nothing, heard nothing, and knew nothing about the death of Superman. They were more than innocent; they were apologetic that they had nothing to offer to help the investigation along, nothing that would bring the killer or killers to justice. They were upstanding citizens, after all.

Blunt, who had a way of summing things up in few words, cleared his throat and turned to Grave. "Well, that just about made me puke."

Grave had to laugh. "Yeah, what a cluster."

"All the fine young innocents."

"Indeed."

"So, what now?"

Grave was torn. He knew they should go back to the station and sort things through with Captain Morgan and the other teams, but his first instinct was to go to the Crab Cove Cinema Cemetery and have a chat with his friend Victoria, who though not alive, knew a lot about the comings and goings of the dead. Perhaps she had already spoken with Superman. If so, they could wrap up this case in an instant.

Still, to go to the cemetery meant dragging Sergeant Blunt along, and there was no telling how he would react to Grave talking to another invisible being. In the end, he decided on a compromise.

"Tell you what, Blunt. Drop me off at home, so I can pick up my Sprite."

Grave sensed that Blunt was confused. "I may need it for later in the day, in case we need to split up."

"Split up, sir?"

"You know, follow different leads."

Blunt said nothing in reply, but quickly slowed the car to make the turn into Grave's neighborhood.

"Thanks, Blunt, I appreciate it."

"No problem, sir."

"So how is that amazing daughter of yours doing?"

Blunt laughed. His daughter, Rippley, a precocious little girl with the ability to be visible or invisible at will, had been instrumental in helping solve their last case, the murders of Lachlan McLachlan and Wright Orville. "She's fine, sir, although she's a bit disappointed that her testimony will not be admissible in court."

"Yeah, I know. It came too close to entrapment, at least in our DA's mind. So she's back to the everyday play of a little girl?"

Blunt hesitated. "Well, sir . . ."

"What?"

"Well, she's gotten a bit full of herself. Now she wants to be a teacher."

"How is that a problem? Teaching is a noble profession."

"Yes, sir, it's just what she's teaching."

"Oh? And what's that?"

"Invisibility, sir. How to be invisible—or visible—at will."

Grave resisted saying how wonderful it would be if little Rippley could teach Blunt—and for that matter, his wife June, who also suffered from visible cloudiness—to materialize fully. Grave wondered whether he would even recognize him—or her. "Um, so how is that a problem?"

"At first we thought, how wonderful. She can teach us to become visible at will. I'm sure you'd like that, sir."

Grave tried not to smile. "I don't know, Blunt. I'm kind of used to you the way you are. Seeing you fully visible might be a distraction."

Blunt shook his head vigorously. "No, sir, I think that you and everyone at the station would be *relieved* to see me, not distracted."

Grave shrugged. "Perhaps. Anyway, so what's the big problem?"

"Well, sir, she got into a discussion of invisibility with June, who called Rippley's process of switching back and forth from visible to invisible *Causal Visibility* and Causal Invisibility."

"Causal? Sounds a bit technical, but so what?"

"So, the fancy terms just gave Rippley even more incentive to teach."

"I don't understand."

"She's set up a school, sir, a school for her visible little friends. We saw the sign on her bedroom door this morning, sir. *The Rippley Blunt School of Casual Invisibility.*"

"Casual?"

Blunt chuckled. "She got the spelling wrong."

"Casual invisibility, huh? I don't know, I kind of like that. In fact, if I were her student, I'd prefer it. *Causal* sounds a bit stuffy, even hard. But casual? Now, that sounds like fun. That sounds easy."

Blunt nodded. "You may be right, sir. She already has ten kids signed up."

"Very entrepreneurial of her."

"Well, there's that. On the other hand, the flip side could mean no end to the mischief that could ensue."

Grave cocked his head. "Oh, dear, I hadn't thought of that."

"No, sir, and it has me and June near worried sick."

Grave tried to give him an assuring laugh, but it came out more like a cackle. "I wouldn't worry about it, Blunt. This week she wants to be a teacher. Next week she'll want to be an astronaut. Kids change quickly."

Blunt nodded. "If only, sir. If only."

They grew quiet, Blunt making turn after turn. Finally, two more turns later, Blunt slowed the hovercruiser to a stop in front of Grave's house.

Grave stepped out without another word, motioning his drone, Barry, to follow. Then he waved goodbye to Blunt, who nodded in a cloudlike manner, not even casually visible, and sped away in the direction of the station.

Grave watched him go, then turned toward the house and stopped dead in his tracks. His father, Jacob Grave, a retired detective, was on the front porch with his fiancé, Ida Notion, a psychic who had helped Simon in several cases.

What in the world are they doing here?

31

Captain Morgan knew he had made a mistake the second his police hovercruiser had turned onto Main Street. Traffic was heavy, much heavier than usual, and he could see right away what the problem was. He had forgotten about the mayoral debate. "Dammit!"

Rum had still not put two and two together. "What's the problem, sir? A little traffic is all."

"If only. It's the damned mayoral debate, and we're stuck."

"Maybe, sir, but let me out. I'll see if there's a way out of this."

Morgan brightened. "Good idea." He rolled down the window and moved aside so Rum could exit the vehicle. In seconds, the little drone was hovering high overhead, turning this way and that, searching for a likely—and quick—exit.

Morgan pressed the communication button on the console of the hovercruiser. "This is Captain Morgan. We need to exit this street as quickly as possible."

He could hear the speakers turn on, and after a brief period of static, the official voice of the Crab Cove Police, the late actor Morgan Freeman, the one voice designated for police simdroids, drones, and vehicles, came on. "I'm afraid that's not possible, Captain Morgan."

"Oh, and why not?"

"Sensors indicate that we are pinned in on all sides and are capable of no forward velocity."

"Well, can't you just hover out of here?"

There was a brief pause, and then the voice of Morgan Freeman came back again. "You are speaking to a 2048 police hovercruiser, Model 6A. Maximum vertical lift is six inches at our current capacity."

Morgan sighed and put his head in his hands. Of course, he thought, just my luck to draw a 6A from the motor pool. "Sorry, I thought you were a newer model."

"Understood. I hear the newest models can actually *fly.*" There was a wistfulness in his voice.

Morgan thought to respond, but talking to machines was never one of his favorite things to do. They just kept talking far beyond reason, not knowing how to end a conversation properly. If he had responded, no doubt this hovercruiser would have taken him into a conversation comparing the features of flying and just-hovering cruisers.

"Yes, they can fly," he said, quickly turning off the speakers.

He stuck his head outside the side window and looked up. Rum was still hovering high above the traffic jam. "Come on, Rum."

He pulled his head back in and peered through the front window. He could just make out a large stage draped in bunting that had been assembled in front of City Hall. Several people stood on the stage, waving at the crowd. Morgan was certain he could make out the two candidates, Mayor Maura Lee Bancroft and her simdroid challenger, Lester Change.

The sudden sound of Rum whirring back into the hovercruiser startled him. "What the—"

"Sorry, sir, didn't mean to surprise you."

Morgan sat back in his seat. "So we're stuck."

"Yes, sir. I'm afraid even the side streets are jammed. Looks like we'll be here a while, at least until the speeches are over, and probably a good deal longer."

Morgan sighed deeply, trying to control his frustration. He was not a patient man. "Well, then, I say we walk the rest of the way."

"What, to the station?"

"No, Rum, to the debate. I need to talk to the security people. See if their cameras picked up someone dropping Superman's body, and more to the point, someone *else* spiriting the body away to the morgue."

Rum waggled in the air. "Sir, not to make too strong a case for it, but couldn't I just call ahead, see if the security team will have time for us?"

"You could, but no, I want to talk to them personally."

"As you wish, sir."

"Come on, let's get out of here."

Morgan pushed open the door and got out, Rum hovering just behind him.

The shock wave from the blast threw them both backwards and to the ground.

32

"It looks like an explosion," said Detective Loblolly.

The boy behind the counter, all tricked out in his Skunk 'n Donuts shirt and cap, shook his head solemnly. "No ma'am, that's our Sunny Daynut. It's more a pastry than a donut, though. Had to be to make the rays stiff enough."

Loblolly frowned back at him. "I don't see it. Look, see the way those orange and red sprinkles fan out, like an explosion. You should call it that."

The boy stared back at her, unwilling to commit to her suggestion. There simply wasn't anything in the Skunk'n Donuts Customer Service Guide to handle this situation.

"So," he said finally, "would you like one of those?" He held his tongs up and clicked them in the general direction of the Sunny Daynut.

Loblolly shook her head. "No, I don't think so." She turned to Detective Snoot, who was about to lose all patience with her new partner. They had been in the store for almost fifteen minutes, and Loblolly still couldn't decide what she wanted. Not that it wasn't a tough choice. "What should I get?"

Snoot sighed, exasperated. "Well, I know you like Detective Grave, so why not try what he likes."

Loblolly waggled her head from side to side, trying to decide. "Yeah, maybe, but it looks messy."

Snoot laughed. "If you think that's messy, you should see Grave's face after he eats one."

Loblolly frowned. "I don't like messy."

"Then how about just a plain cake donut? No muss, no fuss, and we're out of here."

Loblolly shook her head in a way that suggested no way. "No, too dry. I hate dry donuts."

"Just a simple glazed, then. Everybody likes glazed."

Loblolly continued to shake her head. "No, they make my teeth squeak when I bite in."

Snoot rolled her eyes. "Well, pick *something*."

Loblolly turned back to the case. There were yeast donuts and cake donuts, cream-filled donuts, crab-filled donuts, jelly-filled donuts, bear claws, twists in cinnamon and sugar, and a variety of specialty donuts, including Sunny Daynuts, Morning Sprinkles, and Skunk Tails, a flat, hole-less donut iced in black and white to simulate a skunk's tail.

Loblolly considered each, then dismissed them all, pointing at last at a small bite-sized cruller with a knobby end. "What are those?"

The boy behind the counter beamed. The Skunk 'n Donuts Customer Service Guide had prepared him well for just such a question. He knew the answer by heart, and delivered it in monotone, without inflection or emotion, a rote reply to a frequently asked question. "That's a Little Willy Cruller, named after the founder of Crab Cove, Sir William Skunkford, whose family settled the area as "Skunkford" in 1750 with a modest land grant from the king. The good people of Skunkford had changed the name of the town to Little Willy's Landing shortly after the American Revolution, the name chosen to disparage Mr. Skunkford's legendary anatomical shortcoming as payback for his support of the crown, as well as to encourage his rapid flight. As you travel around town, you will see some variations of Skunk or Skunkford. For example, auto dealer Skunk Ford and its funny slogan, *we smell a deal*. And of course to this very donut shop in which you stand, Skunk 'n Donuts, proud home of the Little Willy Cruller."

Loblolly bent over to get a closer look. "So it's supposed to be his, um . . ."

"Yes, ma'am, and they're just six for a dollar, with or without sugar, cinnamon, or glazing."

Loblolly looked at the glazed ones. "Ewwww."

Snoot had had enough. "Polly, make a decision for Christ's sake. We have work to do."

Loblolly stood back up. "Okay, okay. Hey, wait, what's that one over there?"

The boy was ready. "Those are Crab Claws, one of our bestsellers."

"Okay, I'll have two of those for here and a dozen chocolate donuts to go." She turned to Snoot. "For the squad room." She turned back to the boy. "Oh, and an extra chocolate donut in a separate bag."

Snoot laughed. "Don't tell me. For Grave."

Loblolly waggled her eyebrows. "A girl has her tricks."

Snoot was about to respond, but there was suddenly a loud sound that rattled the windows and shook the building. "What the hell?"

Loblolly turned and pointed out the window. A column of smoke was rising from the center of town. "Isn't that where City Hall is?"

"It is, it is." She turned to the boy. "Hurry up with those donuts, and make them all to go."

33

Detective Grave's first thought was that he had made a mistake getting out of the hovercruiser. He should have just headed back to the station with Sergeant Blunt, leaving his father and Ida standing on the porch with their drones, Bubba and Crystal Ball. But his second thought was that he was already out of the car, and Sergeant Blunt had sped away. There really was no choice in the matter. "So, why are you guys here?"

Jacob Grave, sensing that very question, was quick with an answer. "My TV's on the fritz. Came over to watch the debate on yours, if you don't mind."

Simon shuddered every time he saw his father these days. If Simon was the spitting image of Dudley Do-Right, then his father was the 74-year-old version: withered and hunched, with spindly legs that could barely take him to the bathroom and back. His hair was all but gone, a few white hairs bravely battling on, and his eyes, once a crystal pale blue, were now rheumy and clouded.

Simon knew that what he minded, or didn't, was of no consequence to his father. His father's TV was broken, so he just came. End of story.

"That's fine, dad."

"Good, good," said Jacob, "but hurry. It's already started."

Simon walked up the steps and punched in the door code. "Let me get in first, dad. I don't want Lucky to get out."

Jacob bristled. "Dog, dog, I don't know why in hell you thought it was a good idea to have a dog. You're never home."

They'd had this argument before. Simon liked having a dog to greet him when he came home, particularly this crab hound, a little lap dog that resembled the Luck Dragon in that old children's movie *The Neverending Story*.

"It's fine, dad. He watches TV all day, and besides, he has a drone handler to walk him, feed him, and handle any psychological trauma of life in isolation."

Jacob grunted. "It's criminal is what it is."

Ida, ever the peacemaker, chimed in. "Leave him alone, Jacob. If he wants a dog, he wants a dog."

"Thank you," said Simon. "How are you, Ida?"

Ida squinted at him. "Better than you, I'd say. Don't tell me. There's a new case, a murder, right? Bodies everywhere, and it's a head-scratcher."

Unlike Simon's father, who favored a manner of dress between casual and slovenly, Ida was by comparison, a fashion plate. Today she was wearing a mauve pants suit accented by a buttery yellow scarf tied tightly around her neck to disguise her age. Her brown hair, which she usually kept in a tight bun, was flowing over her shoulders, which helped lengthen her otherwise round, moonlike face. She was not exactly beautiful, with a big nose, large puffy lips, and barely there eyebrows, but her golden eyes had a way of transfixing you, and her voice, deep and husky, had its charms. And apparently, Jacob found her "sexy as hell," a phrase that made Simon cringe.

Simon sighed, hard enough that Ida noticed. "What?"

He was hoping to get in and out of the house and drive away in his Sprite without looping Ida into the investigation. "Yes, there's been a murder, or at least a death, and the body's been everywhere it seems, but I don't have time to talk about it. Have to get to the station for an important meeting."

He pushed open the door slowly to ease his way in and grab Lucky before the little beast could escape to the outside. "Gotcha," he said, trying his best to fend off Lucky's tongue, which was already halfway through cleaning his face.

His father and Ida pushed in behind him, closing the door behind them before Lucky could escape.

"Where's your remote?" said Jacob.

Simon sat Lucky down in a nearby chair. "It's voice activated, dad. You know that."

"Oh, right. What's that code again? Open sesame? Viola?"

"It's Voilà, dad, not Viola."

Jacob chuckled. "I know that, I know that. Jesus, can't a man make a joke?" He spread his arms wide and shouted, "Voilà."

The system came on instantly, but instead of one-wall mode, which Simon greatly preferred, it opened in Surround Vision, images not just displaying on all four walls and the floor and ceiling, but throughout the space. It was as if the three of them, plus Lucky and all their drones were not just watching TV, but were *on* and *in* TV.

For a brief second, they were in an old western, a herd of stampeding cattle heading right for them, but then Simon yelled out, "Debate!" The channel changed and with it the scenery. Instead of being trampled by a herd of cattle, they were being virtually trampled, jostled, and otherwise inconvenienced by a crowd of people in front of a temporary stage outside City Hall.

The shock of it always took Simon by surprise; it took him a few seconds to get used to the experience. Not so for Ida and Jacob, who seemed to delight in it.

"I have to get us one of these, Ida," said Jacob.

"Oh, yes, please," said Ida, clapping her hands like a child begging for an ice cream cone.

"I can turn it back to flat screen if you like," said Simon.

Ida and Jacob looked at him like he was crazy.

"Or not."

"Look," said Jacob, paying Simon no attention. "Here they come. Mayor Bancroft and that simdroid fella, what's his name."

"Lester Change."

"Yeah, him. Les Change. Who does he look like to you, Ida?"

Ida sighed. They'd had this conversation before. "I keep telling you, Jacob, he looks just like Ronald Reagan."

"Reagan?"

"Yes, Jacob, Ronald Reagan, 40th President of the United States, from way back when. How many times do I have to tell you that?"

Jacob bristled. "As many times as it takes. And I still don't get it. Why would a simdroid who looks like a president run for mayor?"

Ida looked over at Simon and shook her head and shrugged as if to say, *what am I going to do with this old man?* Jacob's memory was going, fast.

"Look, dear," said Ida, her voice going soft. "When the Supreme Court gave the vote to simdroids, it caught everyone flatfooted, including Ramrod Robotics. They didn't have time to create a suitable mayoral simdroid, so they converted one from their presidential series. Les Change just happens to be a Ronald Regan model."

Jacob nodded. "I knew that, I knew that."

Ida let it go and changed the subject. "Anyway, Mayor Maura Lee Bancroft has my vote."

Jacob laughed. "Of course she does."

What ensued was a spirited debate on the pros and cons of each candidate, in most cases a complete distortion of their stated policies and the demonstrable facts. Jacob and Ida were voters, after all, and not required to know anything. Elections were never about facts, after all; they were about enthusiasm.

Simon was instantly bored, and turned his attention to the event itself. Bancroft and Change stood behind opposing lecterns, waving at the crowd, which was ten deep around the stage.

Simon turned and looked back down Main Street, which was chock-a-block with cars, including a police hovercruiser stuck like everyone else. As he watched, the door to the hovercruiser opened and Captain Morgan stepped out, Rum at his side.

The sound of the blast made Simon turn back to the stage, which had disintegrated. Spectators were on the ground, some not moving, some struggling to get up.

Simon turned back to Captain Morgan. He was on the ground, not moving.

Simon raced for the door, then stopped, turned back and shouted, "Continue, save recording, high def."

Seconds later he was in his Austin Healey Sprite, barreling out of the driveway, the sound of gospel music filling the air, the volume stuck on eleven.

34

The goal of chaos is order, but chaos plays to its own music, striking out in unexpected directions, like a jazz musician in thrall, hitting notes with wild abandon before settling back into the melody, if only briefly, before striking out again, each riff its own symphony.

So it was with the scene before Detective Grave. The chaos of the blast had past, replaced by the chaos of the aftermath. EMT drones were everywhere, performing triage and tending to the injured. Ambulance drones hovered overhead, waiting for the next casualty, ready to transport them to Crab Cove General Hospital. Reporters, who had been there to cover the debate, instead found themselves trying to make sense of what had happened, their microphones shoved into the faces of anyone they could find. Grave could also make out a score or more of police drones conducting scans of the area for later examination.

He took this in as quickly as he could because the one person he wanted to find was Captain Morgan. Was he hurt? Was he dead?

Grave made his way to the captain's hovercruiser, where he found a small pool of blood, but no Captain Morgan. He wasn't sure if that was a good sign or not. They could have already transported him to the hospital, or the morgue. And Rum was nowhere to be seen among the hovering drones. All that was left of him, to Grave's mind, was the two little cutlasses lying on the ground. Grave bent down and picked them up. "Where are you, Rum?"

The answer came quickly, and insistently, by way of a finger being poked into his back. "Right here, Grave."

Grave spun around. "Captain!"

Morgan pointed at his face, which was a collage of Band-Aids. "Well, yeah, more or less. Quite an explosion, that."

Grave looked above and around Morgan. "So, where's Rum?"

Morgan smiled. "Oh, he's fine. I sent him back to the station."

Grave held out his hand. "I found these."

Morgan was delighted. "Wonderful. We looked all over for them. Rum will be thrilled."

"Good, good," said Grave. "So, shall we set up a perimeter, string some crime scene tape?"

Morgan grunted. "I wish. No, the FBI is already here. It's their show now. I've already sent Loblolly and Snoot and the others home. You know, they got here much faster than you did."

Grave ignored the criticism. "The FBI? Really? How did they get here so quickly?"

Morgan rolled his eyes. "Because they're the frickin' FBI. Who the hell knows? They have a nose for these things, I guess."

Grave frowned. "A shame. I got the whole thing on tape, in Surround Vision."

Morgan beamed at him. "Holy shit, that's great."

"Yeah, I thought so. Anyway, I'll bring it in tomorrow, give it to the FBI."

Morgan looked alarmed. "You'll do no such frickin' thing. Bring it to the station, so we all can have a look."

"But the FBI."

"Screw the FBI. I have a feeling this explosion is related to the death of Superman."

"What? How?"

Morgan shook his head. "*Instincts*. But never mind that now. We'll discuss it in the morning. For now, go home and get some rest. We'll meet at the station at ten."

35

Claw scanned the men at the table, then shook his head in disgust. "Does anyone know where the hell Pax is?"

Oakie chuckled. "Probably sniffin' 'round that doctor woman."

"That'd be my guess, too," said Fiddler. "Seems he spends more time at the hospital than anywhere else these days."

"Shit," said Claw. "This will not end well."

"I don't know," said Jerry Lee. "Met her once. Seems nice, certainly beautiful."

Claw sighed. "All right, let's get to it. Can't wait around all day for the boy." He turned to Jerry Lee. "What's the damage?"

Jerry Lee cleared his throat. "Nothin' that can't be fixed."

"Such as?" said Claw.

Jerry Lee could see Claw wanted all the details. "All right, all right. The rotating crab on top of the truck took a beating. Lost a claw. And the windshield took a few hits. We'll have to replace that. And, of course, with all the smoke and flying shit, we had to toss a couple hundred bucks of crab and such."

Claw puffed out his cheeks. "But you're okay?"

Jerry Lee nodded. "Pretty much. Still have a little ringing in my ears, but you know, still in one piece."

"How about Smoothie. He okay?"

"Yeah, he's fine." Jerry Lee began to chuckle.

"What?"

"The boy pissed his pants pretty bad."

Everyone laughed.

"Well," said Crabs, trying his best to talk over the laughter. "There are prospects and there are prospects. Some of these roe boys turn out to have soft shells." He turned to Jerry Lee. "What do you think? Is Smoothie hard enough?"

That comment brought even more laughter, which went on for some seconds before Claw gaveled it down. "Enough, enough."

He turned back to Jerry Lee. "See to the damage and work with Sookie on the costs."

Jerry Lee nodded.

Claw started to change the subject, then reconsidered, turning back to Jerry Lee. "So, the mayor and the challenger are both dead, right?"

Jerry Lee frowned. "That's the damndest thing about it. Overheard an FBI agent after the blast. Apparently, they're both fine. Seems the feds added an extra level of security at the last minute."

"What? What are you talking about? We all saw the blast. No way anybody walks away from that."

Jerry Lee shrugged. "That's the thing, though, isn't it? They weren't there. Just holographic images."

Claw's mouth dropped open. "What the—"

36

There's something to be said for chocolate donuts, but in Grave's experience it usually went something like, "Why are there no chocolate donuts?"

The boy behind the counter, who had apparently fielded that very question many times since the explosion at City Hall, tried his best to calm Grave's concern through diversion. "We here at Skunk 'n Donuts pride ourselves in satisfying our customer's needs and desires. However, there are times, through no fault of our own, when demand for one or more of our tasty treats far exceeds supply. Such is the case today. Apparently what people want most after an event like today's bombing is donuts, and chocolate, I'm afraid, is their go-to choice."

Grave could tell by the way the boy delivered the bad news that he was mostly relying on a prepared statement, probably from some ill-conceived employee manual. "Well, then, when do you expect a new supply?"

The boy frowned in a way that suggested a deeper apology was on the way. "I'm afraid not until tomorrow morning. If you get here at seven, there should be plenty."

Grave sighed in defeat, which apparently was in the employee manual.

"May I make a suggestion?" said the boy.

"Of course."

He pointed at the only donuts left in the shop, three partial trays of Little Willy Crullers, one each for sugar, cinnamon, and glazed. "Those are Little Willy Crullers, named after the founder of Crab Cove, Sir William Skunkford, whose family settled the area as Skunkford—"

Grave held up a hand. "Stop, I know what they are and I know who he is."

The boy looked chagrined. "They're quite tasty."

"No thanks." There was no way Grave would have anything to do with a donut inversely proportional to William Skunkford's shoe size. "I'll just come back at seven."

"Good idea," said the boy as Grave turned and walked out of the shop. He didn't have the donut he wanted, but he did have an idea. As much as he wanted to review the Surround Vision of the incident, the idea of finding his father and Ida still there put that thought aside.

No, he would pay a visit to his friend Victoria Skunkford at the Crab Cove Cinema Cemetery. Although the little girl, daughter of Sir William, was no longer alive, she was nonetheless a good conversationalist.

And she knew things. As the resident guide and docent for the recently deceased, she might already have welcomed Superman into the fold. In Grave's experience, dead people sought their final resting place, even before they came to rest. And if that was the case for Superman, the whole investigation might be solved in a minute.

Ten minutes later, he and his drone, Barry, were walking and cruising up the path to Victoria's favorite bench.

Barry was trying to dissuade him from his plan. "Sir, I know you think you see this little girl—what's her name?"

"Victoria."

"Yes, Victoria. Really, sir, it's quite alarming to see you talking to nothing and no one."

Grave chuckled. "What? I do that every day with your namesake, Barry Blunt."

Barry sighed. "It's not the same, sir."

Grave jabbed his finger at Barry, who whirled away. "Listen, Barry, I see dead people, or at least some dead people. Ida thinks I'm an empath or a sensitive or something. In any case, I can see Victoria and she can see me, and our conversations are always valuable, particularly in regards to murders and murder victims."

Barry relented. "As you wish, sir, but if you don't mind, I'll just buzz over to Bendigo Bottoms' grave. I hear he has a new wholly holographic display now."

"Really?" said Grave. "I'll have to check that out later. Yes, go on, I'll come find you when I'm done. And give my best to the reverend."

Barry pitched up and down to signify *yes*, and sped away back down the path.

Grave looked up the path to Victoria's bench, and there she was. The little girl, forever ten years old, was always a delight to see, from her red hair and freckles to her simple gingham dress. Everything about her shouted eighteenth century.

She spotted him at once, and waved with glee. "Oh, hello, Simon. So good to see you again."

"And you," said Grave, sitting down beside her.

She could not suppress a giggle. "I *know* why you are here."

Grave was about to speak, but she put a finger to his lips. "No, no, do not tell me. It is about Superman, is it not? And might I say, what a strange name for a man."

Grave was stunned, and delighted. "Yes, yes, is he here already?"

"Indeed. In orientation at the moment, but I had a chance to talk with him. Not in any depth, mind, but he was more than willing to share his plight."

"Yes, he was murdered, but we don't know how or by whom."

Victoria nodded. "Yes, I know. I knew you would want those answers, but I have to say, he was being very mysterious about his demise. I did not learn a single thing."

"Oh," said Grave, disappointed.

"No, all he wanted to talk about was how ironic it was, his death."

"Ironic?"

"Yes, and he was quite confusing."

"Oh?"

"Yes, he said his murder was like a black fly in your chardonnay."

As much as Grave loved his chardonnay, particularly Duct Tape Chardonnay, *the wine that can fix anything*, he knew what she had just said wasn't ironic. "What?"

"Exactly, not irony at all. Just misfortune. And when I expressed my opinion, he said, well then, his death was like a death row pardon two minutes late. Again, just bad luck, and sad."

"But he didn't mention any details about his actual death and how that might be ironic?"

She shook her head. "I do not think he understands irony. Every example he gave was just sad, random, or annoying, but none was ironic."

Grave nodded. This discussion wasn't getting him anywhere. "Back up a minute. Did he mention the Sons of Irony or going to their clubhouse?"

Victoria frowned. "Sadly, no. All he seemed interested in was that explosion over at City Hall."

"You heard it?"

"Of course, I have full aural faculties, as you well know."

"Right, right, so why was he so interested in that?"

"The explosion happened while we were talking, so the first thing out of his mouth was, 'I hope you have room for one more.'"

"One more?"

"Yes, exactly what I asked, and he said, 'Why, the mayor, of course.'"

"Wait," said Grave, trying to catch up. "So Superman, who is dead, knew about the coming explosion?"

Victoria giggled. "He did. Is that not something? Oh, and he was quite surprised when I told him no one was killed. In fact, he seemed quite confused."

Grave's mouth dropped open. "Well," he said finally, "I guess that really was a black fly in his chardonnay."

37

A squad room is like a canary in a coal mine. If something terrible has happened or if something spectacular has happened, you need only look at the demeanor of the people and simdroids in the room to know that something significant has happened.

What confused Grave when he walked in was that everyone seemed preternaturally happy and upbeat. Surely after the explosion, the canary should have been singing a more somber, serious tune. But everyone was joking around and moving about the room in a way that suggested they had just won the lottery.

And then Grave saw it, and the mystery hit him full force. A Skunk 'n Donuts box, once the proud protector of a dozen chocolate donuts, sat empty next to the coffee bot, which was in the robotic act of brewing up a fresh pot of coffee. That in itself was an oddity. The bot pot was always empty.

The voice of Sergeant Barry Blunt startled him. "Sorry, sir, you just missed it. Detective Loblolly bought a dozen chocolate donuts for the team. I'd forgotten how wonderful they are."

Grave sighed. "I don't suppose you saved one for me."

Blunt seemed nonplussed at the oversight. "Oh, oh, I guess I should have. Just didn't think about it, sir."

Grave nodded, resigned to another day free of chocolate donuts. He scanned the room. A lot of happy patrolmen, but no detectives, and he could see that Captain Morgan's office was empty and dark. "So, where is everybody?"

"In the conference room."

"Why not the captain's office?"

Blunt shrugged. "Beats me. Just what the captain wanted."

Grave glanced at his watch. "Come on, it's time."

They walked into the room, which was filled with detectives: Charlize, Smithers, Loblolly, and Snoot, with the captain at the head of the table. No drones, of course. The captain wouldn't want to be interrupted. And Grave also noticed there was no canary in this room. It had a seagull named Horace.

Grave blinked at the sight. "What's he doing here?"

"Ah, there you are," said Captain Morgan. "Horace here said he had something to say." The captain shrugged. "So . . ."

Grave accepted the non-explanation. "Well, why not?"

"Exactly," said Morgan. "Now, do you have the Surround Vision thingy?"

Grave pulled the tiny disk out of his pocket and held it up for all to see. "I do."

"Great," said Morgan. "As you know, this room is equipped with Surround Vision capability. Couldn't do this in my office. So, Grave, hand it over."

Grave dutifully handed the disk to Morgan, who instantly handed it to Detective Loblolly, who quickly inserted the disk into a small slot in the wall and turned off the lights.

"Wait," said Grave. "Lights back on, please."

Morgan was a bit befuddled. "What now, Grave?"

He knew he was taking a risk, but he proceeded anyway. "According to Victoria—"

Morgan slammed his fist on the table. "No, not the ghost thing again. Really?"

"Sir, please," said Grave. "I know you are skeptical." He looked around the table. "Perhaps all of you are skeptical, but the fact is I can see dead people, or at least some dead people, Victoria being an important one."

Morgan sighed, resigned to it. *An invisible girl, a talking bird, and now this, a ghost,* he thought. "Okay, okay, but make it quick. We need to analyze the Surround Vision thingy."

"Thank you, sir. When you hear what I have to say, I'm sure you'll understand its importance. You need to hear this to put the Surround Vision, um, thingy in perspective."

Morgan groaned. "Get to it, Grave."

"Yes, sir." He moved to the table and sat down next to Blunt. "It seems Superman knew about the explosion before he died."

Captain Morgan's eyes grew wide. "I knew there had to be some connection. I knew it!" He motioned Grave to continue.

"Right," said Grave. "So, anyway, when Victoria and Superman's ghost heard the explosion, Superman told her to expect one more ghost—the mayor."

Morgan whistled through his teeth. "So he must have been involved somehow." He had a sudden realization. "And maybe that's why the SanniClaws dropped his body at City Hall."

"Wait, what?" said Grave.

Morgan shook him off. "Just a theory, just a theory. We'll get to that. Go on, did you learn anything else from, um . . ."

"Victoria. Yes, yes I did. Superman said his death and dying at the Sons' clubhouse was somehow ironic."

Morgan looked puzzled. "Ironic?"

Snoot spoke up. "You know, sir, like rain on your wedding day"

"Or a free ride when you've already paid," said Loblolly.

"Wait," said Charlize. "That's not irony."

"No," said Smithers. "That's just sad and unfortunate."

"Hmm," said Snoot. "What about free advice that you just didn't take."

"Not irony," said Charlize.

Grave jumped in. "Superman said it was like a black fly in his chardonnay or a death row pardon two minutes late."

Charlize and Smithers looked at each other, then spoke as one. "Not irony."

Morgan groaned. "Forget irony, Grave. Anything else?"

Grave shook his head. "No, sir. We can watch the Surround Vision now."

Morgan motioned to Loblolly, and the room went dark.

38

Claw didn't like to be in the dark—about anything. The price of crabs. The maintenance schedule for his food trucks. The exchange rate between American dollars and Martian musks. The precise softness of a softshell crab. Anything. He was a claws-on manager, and didn't like to be blindsided by news he should have known.

He was also quick to anger, and turned on the closest available victim, in this case Jerry Lee, the messenger. "Holographs? Holographs! What, am I the last person to know about this? The mayor's *alive*, and I'm sittin' here thinking she's *dead?*"

Jerry Lee knew he was in trouble, but he also knew the best way to approach Claw when he was in one of his moods was to just ride it out. Take the shots to the head while backing the fight up to a safer place. "Sorry, boss. Things have just been happening so fast. I thought you already knew."

"Knew? Shit, I'm sittin' here thinkin' the world has come to an end. I mean, hell, what would we do without the mayor? She's been our key to the golden ticket."

Jerry Lee nodded. The money laundering, the black-market shipments of crabs to Mars. The Old Bay spice trade. The whole frickin' megillah. "Exactly, exactly, boss, but really, truly, I thought you knew."

Claw puffed out his cheeks, a sure sign to Jerry Lee that the worst was over. Whatever steam Claw had built up, he was now releasing it in almost visible puffs, the news that the mayor was still alive mollifying the effects of not knowing she was alive.

"Okay," said Claw, turning to the others at the table. "We've lived to fight another day." He looked at each one in turn. "But only just barely. I want to know who did this, and I want to know *fast*."

He slammed the gavel down on the table, and everyone scrambled for the door.

39

There's something to be said for Surround Vision. It's wonderfully immersive, for one thing. You actually feel like you're there, wherever there is, and not where you are, which in the case of Detective Grave and the others, was an otherwise stuffy conference/interrogation room at the Crab Cove Police Force's one and only station.

The second thing that can be said about Surround Vision is that everyone comes at it from a different perspective. Whereas in flat-screen mode, every viewer pretty much sees all that's happening, all at once, Surround-Vision mode is infinitely more complex. Viewers have a 360-degree view available to them, so some will look 90 degrees, while others look 60 degrees, while still others spin in place, not sure where to look first.

So it wasn't until the sixth time through the blast scene tape that everyone pretty much agreed on what they had just seen six times. First, whoever planted the bomb under Mayor Bancroft's lectern knew what they were doing; the blast was fierce, but it was also controlled, the main force of the blast directed directly upward so that the mayor would take the full brunt of the blast, and not the crowd.

"This bastard knew what he was doing," said Captain Morgan, and everyone nodded in agreement.

The second thing was there was a second bomb, one placed under the simdroid candidate's lectern, which only partially detonated, and only because the first bomb had gone off first.

"It would not be like this person to screw up on the second bomb," said Morgan. "The first bomb went off precisely when the two of them, albeit holographic two-of-thems, stepped behind the lecterns. No, I think we might be dealing with two bombers, one who hated the mayor and one who hated her challenger."

Some nodded in agreement, some shook their heads in disagreement (two bombers? Really?), but in either case, Morgan's statement brought them to the third thing.

Grave had noticed it first, a little detail missed by everyone through five viewings of the tape. He had to freeze the action and point out what he saw before the gasps came from the others in the room. They were looking at the club vest, or cuts, of none other than Superman, president of the Krypto Knights. The interesting thing was that they were being worn by a person known to all of them: Crab Cake Johnny, Crab Cove's ever-wandering homeless person, an annoyance to tourists and citizens alike.

"It's Crab Cake Johnny, all right," said Morgan. "So *how* did he get those cuts?"

"And *when?*" said Grave.

"And *where?*" said Charlize.

"And *why?*" said Loblolly.

"And from *whom?*" said Snoot.

"And, um," said Blunt, "what's left?"

"*What,*" said Grave.

"Yes, what?" said Blunt.

"*What,*" said Grave again.

Charlize held up a hand to shush them both. "Stop, what Grave is saying, Sergeant Blunt, is that *what* is the last item in the who-what-when-where-why-and-how measure of journalistic thoroughness, the elements of a story that make it a story, or at least newsworthy."

If they had been able to see Blunt's face clearly, they would have seen him blush. As it was, they just heard him say, "Oh."

Blunt's embarrassment was short-lived, however, because ME Jeremy Polk, who had joined the team in a burst of outside light between the fourth and fifth viewings, spoke up. "I can help with some of those questions, or at least I have a theory."

"Well, go on then, man," said Morgan.

"First," said Polk, "let's discuss the results of the autopsy."

"The floor is yours," said Morgan.

Polk began pacing. "Superman bled out from multiple knife wounds, between 2:00 a.m. and 4:00 a.m. I'm sure you can nail that down if you just time-check his calls."

"3:45 a.m. and 3:52 a.m.," said Snoot.

"Well, then, that's *when* he died, or thereabouts, but there's the question of the process. How long it took him to bleed out."

"Right," said Charlize. "That would depend on the wounds. How many? Where? Their length and depth. And, of course, whether he was taking blood thinners and so on."

Polk rolled his eyes, annoyed. "May I continue, detective?"

Charlize shrugged. "Yes, of course."

"Cutting to the chase, Superman was killed by a tiny blade, the kind you'd find in a multi-tool, a tool quite useful, I would think, in making and placing a bomb."

"Sounds like a logical leap," said Morgan, a frequent leaper.

Polk shook his head. "Not when you consider that Superman's wounds contained traces of red, blue, yellow, black, and white insulation from electrical wire—the very colors used in most bombs."

"Wow," said Loblolly.

"Indeed," said Polk. "Further, the wounds also contained traces of explosive chemicals. I'll spare you the chemical names, but suffice to say, they are the kind used by professionals."

"So," said Morgan, "you think Superman happened upon a man placing a bomb?"

"Yes, that certainly makes sense," said Polk.

"And," said Charlize, "if that's the case, why was Superman even there?"

"Perhaps to place his own bomb," said Smithers.

"The one that didn't go off," said Grave.

"Maybe," said Polk. "We'll have to get some cooperation from the FBI on that one."

Morgan grumbled, almost growled. The last thing he wanted was to deal with the FBI, but he knew he'd have to do it anyway. "I'll see to that."

"Anyway," said Polk, resuming his pacing, "Two more things. First, given the nature of his wounds and the parameters Charlize has so helpfully laid out for us, Superman had perhaps just enough time to make it to the Sons' clubhouse."

"I don't get it," said Snoot. "If someone had knifed me, the first thing I'd think of was calling for help or even trying to make it to the hospital."

"And a hovercycle is faster than waiting for an ambulance," said Grave.

"Right," said Snoot, turning to Polk. "So, did he have time to get to the hospital?"

Polk frowned and looked at the ceiling, in deep thought. "Um, *maybe.* The clubhouse and the hospital are pretty much in a direct line with one another. And those hovercycles are pretty fast."

"Interesting," said Morgan. "So he could have been headed there, but stopped at the Sons' clubhouse instead."

"Yes," said Charlize. "He may have thought he couldn't make it all the way to the hospital, so he settled for the clubhouse."

Loblolly rolled her eyes. "And calls the police—*twice*—to tell them where to find his body? But doesn't identify his killer? I'm sorry, but that's just weird."

Morgan nodded. "It is, but it is what it is. I've listened to Rum's tape of the call, and there's no mention of the killer's identity." He turned to Polk. "Anything else, Jeremy?"

Polk gathered himself up and launched in to his analysis once more. "Second, the wounds also contained traces of leather, and I think you'll find they match the leather from Superman's club vest."

"They call them cuts," said Snoot.

Polk couldn't help chuckling. "Sounds appropriate given the situation, don't you think? Now, back to our Crab Cake Johnny. If those really are Superman's, um, cuts he's wearing, we need to find him. There might be further evidence. Fingerprints, DNA, and such."

Grave turned to Morgan. "Sir, if I may, I know Johnny well. Let me and Blunt have a go at him. Check out his usual haunts."

Morgan nodded. "Good idea."

"Now," said Polk, "the really odd thing about all of this is why Superman would have left behind his jacket."

"I'll take a go at that, if I may," said Charlize. "So, a theory. Our killer stabs Superman, and thinking him dead, removes the cuts and places them near the bomb to point suspicion at Superman and the Krypto Knights. Then, after playing dead, Superman heads for the hospital, then opts for the Sons' clubhouse, then makes his call, and ultimately dies, thus beginning the shuttling of the body from one club to the next, subsequently ending up here." She suddenly stopped. "And then it somehow inexplicably ends up naked at the morgue."

"Wait," said Blunt. "Why not just leave Superman's body there. Why take off his cuts? Or consider this. What if the killer came back later to make sure everything was set, and discovered that Superman's cuts were gone, but his body, to the killer's mind, was still there."

"I don't follow," said Morgan.

"Sir," said Blunt, "to the killer, the only thing that changed was probably the location of the body. So with the cuts gone, he needs something else to tie the Krypto Knights to the crime. So he strips him, sir, and drops the body off at the morgue."

"So he might be viewed as John Doe, at least for a time."

"Yes," said Charlize. "That all makes sense, sort of. Although I think we're all off the mark somehow. Anyway, back to Johnny. He takes the cuts, thinking them a great find, then probably beds down for the night under the stand. Next morning, he's just another man in the crowd when the bomb goes off."

"Could be," said Morgan, "but that's just one possible scenario. And there's still the mystery of the two bombs. Who planted which? And why?"

"Maybe Johnny can help us with that," said Grave. "He could have seen the whole thing go down."

Morgan nodded. "Okay, you and Blunt head out."

Horace the Seagull, who had been unusually quiet during the discussion, not once squawking for French fries, suddenly cleared his throat. "I can help with this, captain."

Morgan squinted at him. "What?"

"Help," said Horace. "Detective Grave here may know Johnny's haunts, but I'd say I know him better."

"And why is that?" said Grave.

"Seriously? Why, he's a competitor. A trash picker. A consumer of discarded French fries. *My* French fries. I have to keep an eye on him, don't I?"

"So, what do you propose?" said Morgan.

Horace smiled as only a seagull can smile, which of course is not at all. Still, the way he cocked his head suggested he was smiling, wryly. "I'll find your Johnny in exchange for a tub of French fries."

Morgan shrugged. "How do we know you just won't fly away?"

"A valid point, but then again, to paraphrase a great poet, *freedom's just another word for nothing left to chew*. No, you needn't worry about me just flying away. I'd do most anything for a guaranteed bucket of fries."

Morgan shrugged. "Okay, okay, take him along with you, Grave."

"No," said Horace. "Grave and Blunt will proceed in their hovercruiser, whilst Blunt's drone, Object, accompanies me in the sky. When I spot Johnny, Object can transmit a message to Grave's drone, Barry." He looked back and forth between Morgan and Grave. "Sound like a plan?"

40

Claw gaveled the meeting to order, but took his time beginning. First, he wanted to look each and every one of them in the eye to see if he could detect even the smallest indication that they weren't being straight with him. The death of Superman had upset the balance in the relationships between and among the hovercycle clubs, and Claw knew the Sons only had a short time to assert their dominance. If they didn't, one of the other clubs would rise; or worse, one of the powerful clubs from the mainland would seek advantage. *Shit*, he thought, *maybe even those bastards The Merry Punsters.* The thought sent shivers up his spine. He hated the Punsters, not to mention their constant stream of bad puns.

His eyes finally settled on Pax, who looked nervous. "What's with you? Where you been all this time?"

Pax did his best to shrug off any concern Claw might have. "Nowhere, everywhere."

Claw smirked. "Come on, it's that doctor, isn't it?"

Pax looked down at the table. "Yeah, a bit."

Claw laughed. "A bit? Shit, man, you look like your chest is filled with Cupid's frickin' arrows."

Everyone laughed, perhaps too heartily for Claw, who gaveled them down. "Quiet." He looked around the table to make sure their smiles had faded, then turned back to Pax. "So you were at the hospital when this bombing went down?"

Pax shook his head. "No, earlier, middle of the night, and then again after the blast, but Lara was pretty busy, so . . ."

"Ah, *Lara* is it?"

"Yes, um, Doctor Hill."

Claw nodded silently, drumming his fingers on the table and looking at the ceiling. "Okay, so you got the hots for the doc. That's fine, just keep her away from here, okay?"

"But—"

Claw jabbed a finger in Pax's direction. "No buts, son. This is not up for discussion."

Pax was seething, but said nothing.

"Now," said Claw, "what *is* up for discussion is two things. One, how in hell did Superman end up on our doorstep? And B, who in hell bombed that debate stage? Dollars to donuts, the Feds are going to try to put this on our doorstep, just like Superman's body, so the more we know, the faster we know, the better."

He looked around the table. Fiddler was waving his hands, which would be a sign of seeking attention for most people. But with Fid it was hard to tell. His hands moved constantly.

"You have something to say, Fid?"

Fid pulled his hands down and held them together, trying to control himself. As it was, it only led to constant thumb spinning. "I do, yeah. My Charlotte, she had to be there early, you know, to set up her stand."

"She still sellin' sodas on the side?"

"Yeah, Claw, yeah. Every penny helps, right?"

"Right, so she saw something?"

Fid shook his head. "Nah, it was what she *didn't* see. Usually, the place would have been crawlin' with security, even that early, but there was no one. Not even frickin' security drones."

Claw raised his eyebrows. "You don't say? Well, that's interesting."

Jerry Lee jumped in. "Sounds like someone in security knew what was going down."

"Or even set the bombs," said Smoothie.

Claw jabbed a finger at him. "Prospects don't talk at meetings, Smoothie, unless I ask." He turned back to Jerry Lee. "Yeah, but Smoothie has a point."

"Yeah," said Jerry Lee, "but since security decided to use holograms of the two of them, the likely scenario is that there was no security because none was needed. And why would they want to endanger their drones?"

Claw nodded. "Yeah, but still. If they knew for sure something was going down, why not just stop it, find the bombs, and move on?"

Pax raised his hand. "Yeah, but think about it. They may have suspected something might be going down. But it's just as logical that they didn't know exactly what they were facing. Was it a bomb? A sniper?"

Claw cocked his head. "I hear what you're saying, Pax, but no, no. If they didn't know exactly what they were facing, they'd have had security up the yin-yang. The place would have been crawling with security."

Pax nodded. "Yeah, that makes sense. So now what?"

Crabs scratched at his scar, then spoke up. "Pax, word on the street is that no one was killed. You were at the hospital. Is that true?"

"Yeah, not that there weren't serious lacerations and broken bones. So?"

"So, doesn't that sound odd? All those people so close to the stand, and no one gets killed?"

"What's your point?" said Claw.

Crabs looked around the table. "My point is, maybe *no one* was supposed to get killed, not even the mayor or that simdroid dude."

"A warning of some kind?"

Crabs nodded. "Exactly. But why?"

41

Grave and Sergeant Blunt headed out in the police hovercruiser in the general direction of the boardwalk, which was no more than a ten-minute drive from the station. In an emergency, they could have made it in five minutes, maybe less, but since they were awaiting instructions from Horace, they saw no reason to rush.

"So," said Grave, "this school of Rippley's, is it restricted to children?"

Blunt chuckled. "Well, she is trying to teach June and me to be more, um, *apparent*, but yeah, it's mostly kids."

Grave wondered how he would deal with the shock of actually *seeing* Blunt. "Any luck with that?"

Blunt's sigh answered the question. "It's hard, you know. Now, June is a different story. She was able to hold full visibility for three seconds this morning. It was amazing. She has the cutest little nose, and a mole just above her lips. Very sexy."

Grave couldn't imagine that, either. To him, June was a cloud equally impenetrable. "How wonderful for her, and you."

"Yes, yes it is. Now, if I can just get the hang of it, we'll be in business."

Grave didn't know what to say to that. Fortunately, Blunt's drone, Object, began waggling in the air. "Incoming call, sir."

"Accept call," said Blunt.

The voice of Grave's drone, Barry, came on loud and clear. "Target sighted due east of Freddy's Famous Fries, approaching Peeler Street entrance to the beach. Rendezvous there."

"Copy that," said Blunt. "End call."

"Well, that was quick," said Grave. "Maybe Horace does know Crab Cake Johnny better than we do. I would have looked for him at Wade's Wonderful World of Waffle Fries."

"Me, too, sir. Anyway, looks like we've got him in our sights." Blunt tapped a button on the control panel. "Beach, Peeler Street, all speed."

The hovercruiser forced them back in their seats as it picked up speed.

"Whoa," said Grave. "When did this thing get so much pep?"

Blunt laughed nervously. "Indeed, sir. A new upgrade, I suspect."

The world outside blurred, suggesting it, too, was a student in the Rippley Blunt School of Casual Invisibility.

42

The orders were clear enough. Grave and Blunt, along with Horace and the drones, would find and interview Crab Cake Johnny. Simultaneously, Charlize and Smithers would proceed once more to the clubhouse of the Krypto Knights, who if all the investigative team's had learned were true, knew far more than they had been letting on. Captain Morgan, meanwhile, would proceed to City Hall for a sit-down with his counterpart in the FBI, and perhaps the mayor, to share and gather information. The two crimes were clearly connected, and the FBI would have to be more forthcoming with what they knew, when, not to mention who, where, why, and how.

That left Snoot and Loblolly to "hold down the fort," an order that did not sit well with either of them.

"It's not fair," said Loblolly after several minutes of seething. "Why are we stuck here? We should be out there, collecting evidence."

Snoot, who was on a softer boil, nodded. "Yeah, but what evidence?"

Loblolly took up the challenge. "Well, the relationships between the clubs for one thing. I mean, it's fine to put a laser focus on Crab Cake Johnny and the Krypto Knights; I get that. But what about the Sons and the Vie Kings."

"And the SanniClaws for that matter," added Snoot. "Yeah, I see what you're saying. Still, it might be important to have Crab Cake

Johnny's insights, not to mention the FBI's, before we go barreling back to the others."

"Yeah? Then why did Morgan send Charlize and Smithers back to the Krypto Knights?"

Loblolly had a point. It would have been better for any further contact with the Krypto Knights to happen after a more detailed understanding of what went down with the bombing. Still, Snoot had learned enough in her time with the force to trust Captain Morgan's instincts. "I think he has a plan."

"Who?"

"Morgan, and don't give me that look. You're new here, and although I must admit the captain doesn't exactly inspire confidence at times, his instincts are usually bloodhound reliable. And I think he has the scent."

Loblolly laughed. She could picture him sniffing the floor of the squad room and then bolting for the door. "Okay, okay, so what do we do, just sit here?"

Snoot chuckled and pointed at Morgan's glassed-in office. "Well, I could resume my search for a drone to replace Goth, and you could take another crack at Mr. Bug."

Snoot was referring to the crime analyzer in Morgan's office, an MRBG 3000, an outdated technology affectionately known as Mr. Bug because of its various shortcomings, the most glaring of which was a success rate in analyzing crimes approaching but not exceeding a coin toss. "I don't know. It's pretty much junk at this point. It would be like resurrecting an imbecile to help us solve crimes."

Snoot shrugged. "What then?"

Loblolly knew what she wanted to do, which was head out immediately for the Vie Kings, to interview them further, find out what connections they had to the mayor, the challenger, or the other clubs. She also knew Snoot wouldn't go along. "First things first; we need to find you a new drone. Gimme that catalog of yours. There are some new models coming out from Ramrod Robotics that are so good I might even trade in my Pine Cone."

"Okay, sister!" She handed Loblolly the catalog which was dog-eared in more than twenty places.

"My lord," said Loblolly. "I see you're a bit indecisive when it comes to drones."

Snoot attempted a laugh, but then stopped. "I miss Goth. She was the best, the absolute best."

"Oh, honey," said Loblolly, "you have no idea. Let me hook you up with a real go-getter. A drone petite but powerful, and as fast as lightning."

"And black. It has to be black."

Loblolly laughed. "Oh, yeah. I'm way ahead of you, girl." She flipped to the back cover of the catalog, where the drone wholesaler placed its new and best-selling drones.

Loblolly held the catalog in front of Snoot's face. "I give you the Ramrod Midnight Special 437XL."

Snoot's eyes went wide. It was like Goth on steroids. "Wow."

Not to be out-wowed, Loblolly's jaw dropped. "Oh, my god."

Snoot almost squealed. "I know, I know, it's so great."

Loblolly shook her head. "No, not that. Not that drone. Superman's drone."

"What?"

"It just came to me. What Charlize and Smithers said in the meeting. Where in hell is his drone and his hovercycle?"

Snoot shrugged. "Dunno, but I'm sure they'll turn up. We have police drones on it right now."

"Yeah, I guess," said Loblolly, shaking her head. "But there's something we haven't done. Something that needs to be done right now. Come on." She got to her feet and almost dragged Snoot out of her chair.

"Where are we going?"

"We need to listen to the tape of Superman's call."

"But we know what he said."

"Do we?"

"Yeah, the captain said there was nothing on Rum's tape about the killer."

"Exactly, but what about the desk sergeant's tape? All we have is what the sergeant *said* he heard. No, we need to listen to *that* tape ourselves, now."

Snoot looked back longingly at the drone catalog. "Can't I order my drone first?"

Loblolly tugged her farther away from the catalog. "No, that can wait. Come on."

43

Detective Grave and Sergeant Blunt had no trouble spotting Crab Cake Johnny. For one thing, he was the only person on the beach being harassed by both a drone and a seagull. And for another thing, he was like a reverse Waldo—he just stuck out, even in a crowd.

His manner of dress, from head to foot, was outlandish in the extreme. He had a surplus Mars mining helmet on his head, complete with oxygen hoses that led nowhere but waggled like elephant trunks when he walked. His pants, the silvery Mylar underwear worn by astronauts, must have also come from the Marsco Surplus Store. And you could just make out a red vest under his purloined Superman cuts, and that covered in buttons, pins, patches, and other flair to be had from the trashcans that lined the beach, the flotsam and jetsam of dissatisfied children.

And his clothing was just the beginning. He was rail thin and walked with a decided limp, probably from the nonmatching footwear, one a sandal, the other a Martian miner's boot. His hair was white, as was his long, scraggily beard, although the beard was stained yellow and red around his mouth, the result of ketchup and mustard left to dry to a condiment crust. A mouth forever screwed up into a sour expression and pale blue eyes frozen in an appraising squint completed the picture of a man whose life revolved around the beaches and trash cans of Crab Cove.

Of course, if you closed your eyes, you'd know you were close to Crab Cake Johnny fifty feet before you actually came upon him. He smelled of rancid crabs, fries, and sweat. Just moving his arms sent out wave after wave of stench.

And he was waving his arms, briskly, at Horace. "Get this bird the hell away from me."

Horace screamed back at him. "Thief! Stealer of French fries! Malodorous miscreant!"

Grave stepped in. "Back off, Horace, that's enough."

Horace lifted into the sky, but not before offering one final comment. "Pitiful, putrescent purloiner!"

Grave yelled up at Barry. "Take him back to the station."

Horace screamed back. "What about the fries?"

Grave rolled his eyes. "And get him some fries."

"The big bucket?" cried Horace.

"The *biggest* bucket," said Grave. He turned back to Crab Cake Johnny, who was still incensed and shaking his fists at Horace. "We need to have a little talk, Johnny."

Johnny turned to face Grave, his eyes still afire. "About what, asshole?"

Grave grabbed him by the shoulders and shook him. "About these cuts."

Johnny's eyes went wide and then softened. "Oh, it's you, detective. How's tricks? Haven't seen you in a while."

Grave released him. "No, you haven't, which is a good thing, right? Now, about those cuts."

Johnny nodded. "Yes, let's talk about these cuts. Fairly got, at risk to my very life." He pointed at small cuts and nicks on his face. "That bomb—did you hear it?—got me here and here and here."

"No, Johnny, not those cuts. The cuts you're wearing."

Johnny looked down, not understanding. "What?"

"The biker vest, Johnny, the vest. Where'd you get it, and when?"

Johnny blinked, then screwed his face up into an arch frown. "Got it fair and square. Rights of salvage, sir. Rights of salvage."

Grave looked around. They were beginning to draw a crowd of curious beachgoers. He spotted a bench twenty yards away next to one of the beach's showering stations. A young, bikini-clad woman was showering off sea water, her body glistening in the sun.

I need a woman in my life, thought Grave. "Come on, Johnny, over to the bench." He grabbed Johnny by the elbow and marched him to the bench.

Johnny looked around as they walked. "Is that cloud with you Sergeant Blunt?"

"Yes," said Blunt. "How are you, Johnny?"

Johnny looked down at his elbow. "Apprehended, apparently."

"Not to worry," said Grave. "Just have a few questions for you. But first, off with the vest."

Johnny reluctantly complied. "Seriously? What use is it to you? Tattered and filled with holes, it is, and bloody. Or at least it used to be. Gave it a good scrub with sand. Now it's a fine garment, just what Johnny needs to take the night's chill away."

Grave cringed at the word scrub. "You shouldn't have done that, Johnny. This vest is evidence, of a murder."

Johnny turned away and crossed his arms. "I seen nothin'."

Grave shook his head. "Come on, Johnny, you had to see something. Just tell us where and when you got it, and what you saw."

Johnny uncrossed his arms and looked back at Grave, his body slumping in defeat. "All right, but I did nothin' wrong. Nothin'."

"We know that, Johnny," said Grave.

"Just tell us what you know," said Blunt.

Johnny nodded and dropped down onto the bench with a grunt.

Grave glanced briefly at the showering station. The woman was gone. *I really need a woman in my life,* he thought. "Okay, out with it, and start at the beginning, the first time you saw this vest." He turned to Blunt. "Here, bag it, Blunt."

Blunt took the vest and stepped away, pulling out a large evidence bag from the cloud that was him and inserting the vest with great care.

"All right, Johnny," said Grave. "Out with it."

Johnny looked longingly at the bagged vest, then turned back to Grave. "Time's a tricky thing with me, detective. Every day much like the next." He screwed up his face. "Or not."

"The night before the explosion, Johnny. You happened upon a body, maybe even saw it dumped right in front of you."

Johnny shook his head. "No, it t'weren't like that."

"Then what?"

Johnny puffed out a sigh. "I'd been watching them build that stand for days, waitin' for my chance to sleep under it. Finding suitable accommodations is a struggle out here, as well you know, detective."

"Yes, Johnny. Come on, stick to the point."

"Right. So, on the night before the explosion, the stand was finished. A wonderful structure, I might add. A fine piece of craftsmanship."

"Johnny."

Johnny could sense the impatience in Grave's voice. "Very well. The long and short of it is I come to the stand, hoping to finally find a right fine place to sleep, away from those damned noisy tourists, if you know what I mean."

Grave just stared at him.

Johnny got back to it. "Anyway, I snuck up all quiet like, and sneaky, you know? To avoid the security drones, which had been over the place thick as gulls on French fries."

"The long and short of it, Johnny."

"Yes, yes, I'm getting' to it, sir. Okay, so much to my surprise, and I might add, delight, there's no drones. At all."

"No drones?"

"Yeah, I thought it strange, too. If I'd had the tools, I could have dismantled the stand without so much as a look-see from security. Why I could have—"

"Get to it, Johnny. What did you see?"

"Well, I heard it first. A thumping sound, over and over again, and grunts and moans and screams. Then I came upon 'em. One man hovering over the other who was face down on the ground, not moving."

"Did you recognize them?" said Grave.

Johnny shrugged. "Bikers is all. Both had vests on, so I'm sure of that."

"Could you tell which clubs?"

"Nah, the darkness, you see."

"All right, did you hear them talking?"

Johnny rubbed his ears. "I don't hear so good no more. The one who was standing could have been speaking in a foreign tongue for all I know'd. But I could sense the anger. Venomous, it was."

"Okay, what then?"

Johnny chuckled. "I'm no fool, am I? I hightailed it out of there, quick and silent as I could."

"What, that's it?"

"That part, yes. As I left, I could hear one of them running away, then the sound of a hovercycle starting up. You can't mistake that sound, can you?"

"No, you can't. What next, Johnny? How'd you get those cuts?"

"I'm getting to it, detective. Now, with the sound of the hovercycle, I turned back. Maybe I could still find a great place to sleep under the stand. But then, all of a sudden, I hear another hovercycle start up and speed away. I gotta tell you, that one was moving like a bat out of hell, hell bent for leather, pedal to the metal, he was."

"Okay, they're gone. How did you come by the cuts, then?"

Johnny rolled his eyes. "Persistent, aren't you? Well, all right, then. So, with them gone, I figure I'll bed down for the night, which I does. But then—hell, an hour or two later, maybe—I hear the sound of many hovercycles approaching. It was a roar, I tell you. And then there's the sound of something heavy hitting the ground. And then, poof, the hovercycles are gone."

"So you find a body."

Johnny looks up at Grave, surprised. "You know this already? Why am I telling this story, then?"

"Go on, Johnny. Go on."

Johnny grumbled. "Yes, yes, it was a body, and yes, it was wearing those fine cuts your Sergeant has so neatly wrapped in plastic. And yes, I took it off him. I mean, what use was it to him? I was the one who was cold. Or at least cold in a good way."

"What about the rest of his clothes, Johnny? Did you strip those off, too?"

Johnny did a double take. "Me? Strip him? No way. He was a big man. I'd no use for anything but his cuts."

"Okay, okay, so you left him there? Didn't report it?"

Johnny looked at him in disbelief. "Detective, bodies have a way of being found, don't they? And besides, I heard someone coming, or rather lots of people coming, so I skedaddled out of there quick as a gull with a French fry. One thing I learned after all these years in Crab Cove, you don't want nothin' to do with strangers, particularly at night."

"Strangers?"

"Yeah, but don't ask me who. Could have been fellow travelers, people down on their luck. I don't know, I didn't look back. And that was that. End of story. Now, can I have them cuts back?"

Grave shook his head. "No, Johnny, but how about some French fries?"

Johnny beamed. "With malt vinegar?"

44

Snoot and Loblolly played the tape again and again, but they still couldn't quite make out Superman's last words.

"One more time," said Loblolly.

"All right," said Snoot. She pressed PLAY AGAIN and after a brief pause, the voices of the desk sergeant and Superman could be heard for the seventh—or was it the eighth—time.

DESK SERGEANT: Crab Cove Police. Sergeant Freeman. How may I help you?

SUPERMAN: No, it's how I can help *you*, officer.

DESK SERGEANT: You want to report a crime?

SUPERMAN: Yes, my murder.

DESK SERGEANT: Who is this? You know this kind of prank is—

SUPERMAN: Not a prank. I'm dying. On my way to the Sons' clubhouse. You'll find my body there.

DESK SERGEANT: Sir, tell me exactly where you are now, and I'll send an ambulance.

SUPERMAN: Too late. I'll be at the Sons in five. Be there.

DESK SERGEANT: Sir! Sir! Who did this?

SUPERMAN: (garbled). Ironic, right? Goodbye, officer. Olsen, Plan B.

DESK SERGEANT: Sir, say that again. Sir!

TRANSMISSION TERMINATED.

"Shit," said Loblolly. "I still didn't catch it."

Snoot sighed. "Nor I. Damned hovercycles. You gear down and you get that throaty rumble."

"Yeah, he was clearly slowing down."

"Anyway, we're right back where we started."

Loblolly shook her head. "No, the name of the murderer is on this tape. We just have to eliminate the background noise."

"And you know how to do that?"

"No, of course not, but someone at the FBI might."

Snoot scoffed. "Oh, no. The captain won't go for that."

"What? Don't be ridiculous. The name of the killer is right there. I know it."

"Well, you don't know Morgan. He and the FBI just don't get along. It's almost a blood feud. Goes way back."

"I don't care. Morgan needs to know this, and he has to get their help. I mean, shit, this might be the key to both crimes. The FBI will want to be all over this."

Snoot shook her head. "Suit yourself, but I'd make the call with Pine Cone on the other side of the room if I were you, because the captain's response is going to be loud—very, very loud."

"But I'll be handing him the *key* to the crime."

"Ha! You watch. It will be like you're handing him a dead fish. Listen, girl, you better be ready for some real blowback."

"Yeah, well, so be it. Oh, and I need to call Charlize, too. Maybe she can sort out what Plan B is."

Snoot rolled her eyes. "Well, I'd call *her* first. I'm sure she'd tell you what I told you. This is a mistake."

Loblolly frowned. "Not a mistake. I'm sure I can persuade the captain how important this is."

Snoot rolled her eyes. "Your funeral."

Loblolly snapped at her. "Snoot, go order your damned drone. Pine Cone, come here!"

45

After running a gauntlet of reporters and minor FBI agents, Captain Morgan at last gained entrance to the mayor's office, where a meeting was in progress between Mayor Maura Lee Bancroft and Morgan's old FBI nemesis, Cliff "Bull" Montgomery. It was clear the two of them were startled by his sudden entrance.

"Don't mind me," said Morgan. "Hope I'm not interrupting anything important."

The mayor sneered at him. "What the hell do you want?"

Maura Lee Bancroft was not a pleasant woman, ever, unless you count her frequent appearances on the campaign trail, where she somehow transformed herself into a smiling, affable presence. But here in her office, where she reigned supreme, her sour nature manifested itself. She was otherwise a handsome—some might say beautiful—woman, tall and slim, with blond hair stylishly cropped at the shoulder. Her eyes were a deep blue, as was her eye shadow and her designer pants suit. A turtleneck in a lighter blue hid the wrinkled neck that came with age, which Morgan reckoned was mid-fifties. He wasn't sure.

Morgan tried his best to be cheerful, but her sneer brought him right to the point with no dancing around. "As you know, we've had a murder, and—"

She cut him off. "And a gatdam bombing—directed at *me*."

Morgan cocked his head. "And Lester Change. Yes, I realize that."

She cringed at the mention of her challenger. "That loathsome pile of wire, that despicable droid, that, that—"

"Yes, of course," said Morgan. "And the point is, I think the two crimes are connected."

Agent Cliff Montgomery, who had been trying valiantly to match the mayor sneer for sneer, suddenly started and leapt to his feet. "Connected? How?"

"Well, hello to you, too, Bull."

Agent Montgomery smirked back at him. And the smirk had not changed over the years. Montgomery, if anything, was an FBI man's FBI man, from his suit, to his wire rim glasses, to his graying crewcut. His nickname, Bull, was apt, not because of his physical appearance—he was tall and muscular, but not thick and bullish—but because of his bulldog-like way of working cases. He reached out his hand. "Henry. Always a *pleasure*. Now, what have you got?"

Morgan let the hand hang in the air until Bull pulled it back, glowering at him. This was the hard part. Morgan didn't really want to share anything with the FBI, especially Bull Montgomery. In his experience, there was never much reciprocity. You gave the FBI information and got precious little in return. "We have reason to believe that Superman was on the scene of the bombing."

Montgomery was skeptical, almost dismissive. "Oh, and how would the great Crab Cove Police know that?"

"We have a tape showing the whole thing going down. We know that the mayor and Change were holographic images. We know that there were two bombs, one of which fizzled. We know that the bomb was crafted by a professional, someone who knew his way around bombs. And we know Superman was there."

Montgomery took every word as if he were being sprayed with machine gun bullets. "Okay, okay, I'll give you that, but how specifically do you know Superman was there."

"Yes," said the mayor who seemed taken aback, "how?"

Morgan now had the advantage, so he saw no reason not to take advantage of it. He strode to a nearby chair and poured himself a glass of water from the mayor's personal decanter. Then he turned and motioned the two of them to sit back down, taking a sip of water as they complied. "Wonderful water, mayor. And so sparkly."

The mayor was not used to being back on her heels, and recovered quickly, an arch sneer preceding her words. "Screw the water, Henry. Out with it."

Morgan shrugged. "Okay, two things. First, as I said, we have a Surround Vision tape of the whole incident. And in that tape we saw none other than Crab Cake Johnny."

Montgomery snorted. "Him? That old homeless guy?"

Morgan nodded. "Indeed. And he was wearing Superman's cuts."

"I don't get it," said the mayor. "How does that put Superman at the scene?"

"Point two," said Morgan, pausing to take another sip of water. "Damned fine water. Damned fine. Anyway, I just got a call from Detective Grave, who—"

"Oh, god," said Montgomery. "That guy? Don't tell me he's working this case."

Morgan glared at him. "He is, and I know you have a history with him, but he's a fine detective."

Montgomery rolled his eyes. "Okay, what did Grave have to say?"

"He sort of nailed it down, Bull. Johnny came upon two men fighting under the stage the night before the bombing. They were bikers, Bull."

"Fighting? About what?"

"Who knows, but I think at least one of them was responsible for setting the bombs. And as for Superman, Johnny took his cuts off his dead body, right there in front of the stage that same night."

Montgomery ran a hand through his hair. "Jesus." He turned to the mayor. "It's like I thought."

"What do you mean?" said Morgan.

"What do you want to know?" said Montgomery.

Morgan leaned toward Montgomery. "Everything, Bull. *Everything.*"

46

The thing about interrogations, whether they are conducted in a bare-bulb room or in the guise of a casual conversation, is that you learn a lot about the suspect apart from the crime. You learn their tics and triggers. A blink when they're lying. A word or name that sets them off. And with each interrogation of a suspect, the job of the interrogator becomes easier. There is no longer a need for such elementary techniques like good-cop, bad-cop.

So when Charlize and Smithers settled in at the Krypto Knights council table, she had only to say the words suggested to her by Detective Loblolly, and watch Larry "Kent" Abrams squirm. "What is Plan B?"

And squirm he did. "Um."

"Plan B," said Smithers.

Kent looked down at the table, avoiding eye contact. "Um."

Charlize chuckled. "You know we'll find out."

Kent let out a big sigh and lifted his eyes to meet hers. "All right. No big deal. It's a failsafe of sorts."

Charlize cocked her head. "How so?"

"It's a program we build into all our systems. A way to wipe the slate clean, so to speak."

"And why would you do that?"

Kent was incredulous. "What? You've never heard of cybercrime? We want to protect our proprietary software."

"Plan B."

"Yes."

Charlize drummed her fingers on the table. "And how does it work for, say, a drone or a hovercycle?"

Kent knew where this was headed and looked away. "Um."

"Come on, I won't give away your secrets."

Kent nodded. "Okay, okay. It's really quite simple. You would issue an oral command to the drone, which would lead to a cascade of actions by the drone—whatever you'd programmed in."

"And a hovercycle?"

Kent chuckled. "Hovercycles don't have much in the way of brains, so if you wanted to send the hovercycle somewhere or dispose of it in some way, you'd program that into your drone. That's what we do."

"So you invoke Plan B, and the drone does the rest?"

"Yes, exactly."

She looked down at the table and then back up at Kent. "And what would Superman's Plan B be?"

Kent tried his best to shrug off the question. "I have no idea."

Charlize scoffed. "Come on, Kent, you've worked closely with this man for years. You know what he'd do."

Kent ran a hand through his hair, nervously. "I can only tell you my Plan B. I think he would have done the same."

"Which is?"

"I'd have my drone take the hovercycle as far out into the bay as possible and dump it. Then the rest of the cascade would wipe the drone's memory banks and then shut it down."

"So it, too, would drop into the bay?"

"Yeah, I mean that's what my drone would do. I'm not so sure about Superman's. He didn't share as much as you might suspect."

"I see, I see," she said, wondering whether anyone had built a Plan B into her. "Thank you for your help, Kent. It's been most illuminating."

Kent seemed relieved as Charlize and Smithers stood and began walking to the door. He'd lived to dissemble another day.

But then Charlize turned back and tried a technique used by a fictional detective, one of hundreds programmed into her. "Sorry, one last question. Could someone hack into a drone's Plan B, make it do different things? You know, a different cascade?"

Kent blinked.

47

Sookie knew Claw like the back of her hand, knew him to his bones, so when he dropped the invoices on her desk, she knew something was eating at him. "What's with you?"

Claw shrugged. "Nothin'."

She chuckled. "Don't give me that. Something's bothering you—*big time.*"

Claw sighed and dropped into Sookie's guest chair. "I don't know. The price of crab, I guess."

Sookie put down the invoices she was working on. "The price is up. Good news for us."

"Short term, yeah, but if we have another season like this one, well . . ."

He didn't feel the need to finish his thought. She knew as well as he did that the legendary blue crab was endangered. So much so that their plight had become part of the political debate. Lester Change favored declaring crabs an endangered species, with all the controls that brought. And despite all the pressure he was putting on Maura Lee, it was clear she was moving in the same direction, following the wind of the polls.

"No," said Sookie. "It's not the price of crabs, is it?"

He sighed again, in a nuanced way she recognized immediately. "Are you worried about Pax?"

Claw gave a quick nod. "That doctor woman has her claws in him."

"And what's so bad about that, hon? Everyone wants a doctor in the family, right?"

Claw smirked. "Yeah, well, first I'd like a stepson up to the task at hand, which is being a reliable number two."

Sookie frowned. "And he isn't?"

"He was, he surely was, but not lately. He's making mistakes. Oh, not big ones, at least not yet. But he's clearly distracted."

"And you think she's the distraction?"

Claw threw up his hands. "What, are you blind? He's like walking around in a fog over that woman. You can almost see the little hearts and flowers circling around his head."

Sookie got up from her chair, came around the desk, and threw her arms around him. "Are you really that worried?"

"Yes."

"Then let me have a talk with her, find out what's really going on. Maybe this is just like last time. You know, him just needing to get laid."

Claw laughed. "That was a mess, wasn't it? A simdroid of all things."

Sookie tried not to focus on the sexbot incident. "Look, I'm sure that's all this is. Raging hormones."

"You think?"

"I do, but if I'm wrong, I'll have some friendly words of advice for our sweet, young doctor."

Claw smiled. "Don't be too hard on her."

She bent down and kissed him on the cheek. "You know me, babe. Subtle. Controlled. She won't even know what hit her, babe."

She went back and sat behind her desk. "Now, what do we know about this Superman thing?"

Claw rolled his eyes, then rubbed his hand across his face. "Jesus, it's all over the place. For starters, according to Jerry Lee, Superman just comes into the clubhouse, gives him a funny, shit-eating grin and drops dead, like it was some kind of joke."

"A joke?"

"Yeah, Jerry Lee even thought Superman was faking it, but of course he wasn't."

"So?"

"So, for better or worse, we dropped the body at the Vie Kings, thinking screw 'em, let them deal with the cops."

"Yeah, serves 'em right the way they've been gouging us on the spice."

"Exactly, exactly. But then, not to be outdone, the Vie Kings turn around and drop the body at the SanniClaws, who've been pretty much stiffin' the Kings with the money laundering."

"They're cheats, all right."

"They are. I'm glad we handle our own laundry. Cuts out the middle man."

"So what do the SanniClaws do?"

Claw laughed. "I would have thought they'd just return Superman home. They got no beef with them as far as I know. That would have made sense, but no, they drop the body in front of City Hall of all places."

Sookie shook her head. "No, no, it does make sense."

"What?"

"Yeah, this whole election thing. Brush hates the mayor. His department has been getting the short end of the budget stick the whole time she's been in office."

A light went on for Claw. "Oh, so you think he was trying to embarrass her on the eve of the debate."

"Yeah, something like that."

"Right, but that didn't work out either. Because somehow or other, the body ends up at the morgue, completely naked."

"Naked?"

"Well, that's what we hear, anyway. Naked, stripped. Cuts gone and everything."

"Wow."

"Anyway, after this game of body hot potato, we're right back at the beginning. Superman's dead, and we don't have a clue who did it. And everyone's looking at us."

Sookie sat back in her chair with a sigh. "I can't help thinking the bombing has something to do with this."

"I don't know how. I really don't. That sounds like all politics to me. Someone out to get the mayor."

"Okay, let's talk politics. Who stands to gain from her death? Certainly, not us. We're in each other's back pockets."

"I already talked to her. She knows we had nothing to do with it."

"Does she suspect someone?"

"No, she's as baffled as we are."

"Well, what about the Krypto Knights?"

Claw scoffed. "Nah, they provide security for her. And we don't have a beef with them, either. I mean other than hatin' Superman personally. In fact, we're their best customer when it comes to burner drones."

Sookie nodded. "Well, then, there's always the SanniClaws. Like you said, Brush hates the mayor."

Claw considered the possibility, but then shook his head. "I just don't see it. Say what you will about Brush, he and his boys are straight shooters, I mean, aside from the money laundering."

"Well, if not them, who?"

Claw shrugged. "Maybe that simdroid dude, Lester Change."

Sookie chuckled. "If he were human, I could see it. But a simdroid? No, the Laws of Robotics just wouldn't permit it. And besides, I hear there was a bomb under his lectern as well. No, whoever did this wanted both of them out of the way."

"Maybe, but who stands to gain from that?"

Sookie shrugged. "That, my dear, is the question."

48

The last person Captain Morgan expected to see sitting in his office was Brush. But there he was, the big man giving Morgan a sheepish little wave and a nervous grin from within the captain's glassed-in sanctuary.

Morgan started for the office, but Loblolly intercepted him before he could take more than a few steps. "Sir, any news from the FBI?"

"We'll get to that."

He tried to brush by her, but she was persistent. "I mean help with Superman's call. Are they going to do it?"

Morgan stopped again. He couldn't let her know how angry he was with her. Asking a special favor from the FBI was something he didn't want to do. Still, if the FBI could help identify the name of the murderer, why not? He just didn't like the way Bull Montgomery had savored the request, which gave him one up on Captain Morgan. "Look," he said, grabbing her by both shoulders and moving her out of his way. "We'll discuss all this in a few minutes, but yes, the FBI is on it."

Loblolly nearly leaped in the air. "Yes!"

Morgan rolled his eyes. "Whatever." He scanned the squad room. "Where is everybody?"

Loblolly followed his eyes. The room was mostly empty. Just a few simdroid patrolmen, Horace the Seagull wolfing down French fries from a large bucket, and Barry, Grave's drone, standing watch over Horace. "Um, here and there."

"Where's Grave?"

"In the conference room with Retective Must."

Morgan had to laugh. "She finally got her claws into him, eh?"

"She did. They're going over the McLachlan and Orville murders."

"And how's that going?"

"Not as much screaming as you might expect. Pretty quiet, really."

"How long have they been in there?"

Loblolly glanced at the crab clock on the wall and judged the position of the little claw and the big claw. "Over an hour, sir."

"Hmm, okay, we'll give them a few more minutes to have at each other." He pointed at his office. "Besides, it seems that Brush wants to talk to me." He started to walk in that direction, then stopped. "What about the others?"

"Charlize and Smithers called in. Said they were making a stop at Ramrod Robotics to see June Thursday."

"Blunt's wife? Did they say why?"

"No, sir. It was a quick call."

Morgan glanced around the room once more. "And speaking of Blunt."

"Oh, right." She looked around. "He was here just a minute ago, but I gotta tell you, I don't see him all that well."

Morgan snorted. "Welcome to the club." He squinted at the corner of the room. "There he is, that fuzziness near the coffee bot."

Loblolly looked at the coffee bot and shook her head. "If you say so, sir."

"Yeah, that's him. Okay, so what about Snoot?"

"What? Oh, you must have just missed her. She's outside, testing her new drone."

Morgan nodded absently. "Good, good. Now, I better go talk to Brush. When I give you the high sign, go and collect Snoot. We'll have a lot to discuss."

"Yes, sir."

Morgan turned and walked to his office. He could see Brush getting more and more nervous the closer he got.

The man didn't even give Morgan the chance to say hello. "I didn't mean to lie, Hank."

Morgan closed the door behind him and sat down behind his desk. "Lie? You mean you didn't drop Superman's body in front of City Hall like you said?"

"No, Hank, no. That's true."

"And you did it to embarrass the mayor, right?"

Brush sighed. "You know how she's been screwing with me, Hank. Did you know she cut my budget again, this time by ten percent? Pretty soon I won't be able to order supplies."

"Tell me about it, Brush. We've had cuts here as well."

"It makes no sense, Hank, what with all the extra work coming from the Mars Terminal."

Morgan waved him off. They'd had this conversation before, over beers. "So what is this lie you're talking about."

Brush looked around the office, nervously. "Um, I said I didn't know how the body got from City Hall to the morgue." He sighed. "But I did. I do."

Morgan leaned forward, resting his arms on his desk. "And?"

"You ever see the rats we have around here?"

Morgan knew he had. There were regular rats, large brown ones that seemed to favor the crab-processing plants. And then there were the ones let loose by people protesting the building of the Martian Terminal, two years back. Those were fewer in number, but if you ever saw one, you'd never forget it. The protestors had dyed them red, as a way to illustrate the menace they thought the Mars Terminal would pose for the town, and the larger world. Yes, they had said, we can go to Mars, but what will we bring back? And then they'd released the red rats, big suckers from Newest York, their *Rats from Mars*. Morgan sighed. "Once or twice."

"They're big suckers, right? The red ones, bigger than cats, like frickin' possums."

"Yeah, so?"

"I just couldn't leave him lying there all night, what with those hungry rats around. It just wouldn't have been right."

"So you moved him to the morgue?"

"Yeah, after I left the other SanniClaws at the clubhouse, I doubled back to get Superman."

Morgan shook his head. "Why'd you strip him naked?"

Brush was quick to object, waving his hands in front of Morgan's face. "No, I didn't do that. When I came back, I saw a group of homeless people stripping him."

Morgan sat back in his chair. "Okay, that explains the nakedness. Now what about the fact that the body was washed?"

Brush looked away. "Um, that was me." He shrugged. "You know me, Hank? Always a neatness freak."

"Obsessive-compulsive, yeah."

"Right, so, I just did it."

Morgan drummed his fingers on the desk. "You know that's a felony, right?"

Brush threw up his hands. "What, for washing?"

"For interfering with a criminal investigation. And don't forget moving the body—*twice.*"

Brush looked desperate. "But I've told you everything. Doesn't that count for something?"

Morgan considered the possibilities. Charging him. Not charging him. "It might, Brush. Long as you're willing to cooperate going forward."

Brush was quick to respond. "Anything, Hank, *anything.*"

49

Charlize tried her best to focus on June's face, but it was much like the rest of her: fuzzy and cloudy, like her husband's. But at least there was a cloud to look at, unlike June's daughter, who was born invisible and remained so most of the time.

They had worked their way through the usual prefatory chitchat, even discussed Rippley's progress in teaching June and Sergeant Blunt how to become more visible, but it was now time for Charlize to get down to business. "June, we've just come from the clubhouse of the Krypto Knights. Their new leader, Kent, claims that it's possible to invoke what he calls a Plan B for his drones."

"Plan B?"

"He described it as a cascade of final instructions that once invoked would lead the drone to wipe its memory and, in effect, commit suicide."

June had blinked at the name Kent, then nodded politely as Charlize laid out Kent's interpretation of Plan B. "Well, Kent would know. He used to be a senior programmer here. One of the best."

Charlize blinked at the news. "Oh, why did he leave?"

June shrugged. "I have no idea. Programmers come and go here. They learn all they can learn and then move on. Some set up their own shops. Some go freelance. Some just, um, disappear."

"So this Plan B is a *real* thing?"

June waggled her head. "Yes and no. In the prototype stage, there's a backdoor that programmer's can use to tweak the drone's behavior and capabilities."

"So anyone with the skills could do that?"

"Yes, but only in the prototype stage. Once the prototype was approved for production, the backdoor would be closed, protecting all the software and built-in protocols like the Laws of Robotics, and so on."

"Do no harm to humans."

"Yes, exactly, although . . ." She blinked, hard.

"What?"

"Sometimes, even with the best safeguards, something is not quite right with a new model."

"So?"

"So, we'd have to go back in and fix it."

"Wait, you said the backdoor was closed."

June shook her head. "Well, not exactly. There's a backdoor to the backdoor, if you know what I mean. Every drone has one."

"So Kent could have opened that door?"

June nodded. "And done anything, anything at all."

Smithers, who had been following the conversation without comment, something he did routinely in being Charlize's silent partner, suddenly broke in. "But surely the Laws of Robotics could not be abrogated."

June cringed. "I'm afraid even those would be up for grabs, assuming the programmer was proficient."

"Like Kent and the Krypto Knights?"

"Yes, I'm afraid so. As a senior programmer here, I'm sure he did that several times a year. He'd know everything about the drones and could change them in any way he chose."

"I see," said Charlize. "Let me ask you another question. Does this backdoor to the backdoor exist on simdroids as well? Could someone mess with me or Smithers?"

June's sigh answered the question.

50

Sookie didn't need more than two seconds to see why Pax was so enthralled with Doctor Lara Hill. The woman was a knockout. Tall and shapely, with a great rack and legs that went from here to there and back again. And those eyes. Like emeralds. And her hair. A rich auburn, pulled back into a professional looking bun atop her head. Oh, and her skin. Perfection. Sookie would have paid a plastic surgeon anything to have skin like that. With all that, though, Sookie could see that the doctor was tired and had been crying.

Doctor Hill cleared her throat. "Yes, how can I help you?"

Sookie broke from her reverie. "Oh, right, doc." She held out her hand. "Um, I'm Sally, but everyone calls me Sookie. You know, like the female crab. Not that I'm a crab, mind." *Why am I babbling like this?* she thought.

Doctor Hill stared back at her politely. "Yes, yes, um Sally. How can I help?"

Sookie steeled herself. "It's about my son, doc."

Lara sniffled, then grabbed a tissue and dabbed at her eyes and nose. "Oh, what seems to be the problem?"

Sookie cocked her head. "Um, I think you know."

Lara looked up at her like she was seeing her clearly for the first time. "Oh, my god. You're *his* mother?"

Sookie did her best impression of Vanna White in those old reruns, waving at a new product. "The one and only."

Lara shook her head. "Sorry, you just look too young, and so composed. I don't know how you can keep it together."

Sookie shook her head. "Keep it together? Look, doc, I'm not here to talk about me. I'm here to talk about you and Pax."

Lara looked bewildered. "Pax?"

"Yeah."

Lara sighed, picked up another tissue and began crying. "I'm sorry. I thought you were my boyfriend's mom."

Sookie blinked as quickly as her mouth dropped open.

51

Grave was drained, exhausted, when he followed simdroid Retective Must out of the conference room. The retection had gone about as expected; she thought he had done everything wrong every step of the way. He had failed to use logic, protocols, or even common sense on the case, and so on and so on. And she'd make sure his official record would reflect that. His insistence that despite all that he'd solved the case went on deaf oral receivers.

He began walking to the door, hoping for a do-nothing evening with a bottle of Duct Tape Chardonnay, but Captain Morgan grabbed him by the elbow and turned him around. "Back in the conference room, Grave."

"What?"

"To discuss the case." He turned to the others. "Come on, guys, let's do this."

A minute later they were all seated around the table, Morgan at the head and Grave at the other head, or maybe it was a foot. Grave wasn't sure, and his mind didn't want to deal with the question, anyway.

Morgan cleared his throat. "So, a couple of things, then we'll go around the table, see what you've all got."

He waited until everyone had nodded except Grave. "Grave, are you with us? You look a bit lost down there."

Grave tried his best to sit more erect, to show that he was wholly there (though he wasn't) and that he was ready to participate (though he wasn't). "Yes, yes, please proceed."

Morgan puffed out his cheeks. "Okay, the good news is that the FBI has agreed to share information with us. The bad news is that they know precious little. It's almost as if the explosion never occurred. All the security cameras were inexplicably down, and whoever set the bombs did a complete DNA wipe before they left."

Snoot raised her hand. "Any information on the bombs themselves?"

Morgan nodded. "Indeed. A real professional job. Not some bomb cobbled together with fertilizer and such. No, the bomber used military-grade explosives, and his device, as best as the FBI has so far been able to piece together, was state-of-the-art."

"And yet," said Loblolly. "And yet the second bomb fizzled on him. Doesn't that suggest a lower skill level?"

"Not necessarily," said Charlize. "It could have been quite intentional. One bomb to kill, the other to only wound. Or in the case of a simdroid, maybe to do no harm at all."

"Wait," said Blunt, speaking from the cloudy middle of the table. "Back up a minute. Why did the debate take place with holograms instead of live and in person?"

"A good point," said Morgan. "And why the FBI's response was so quick. They were already there."

He let that sink in and got the raised eyebrows he was expecting. "They'd received an anonymous tip that someone was out to kill, or rather destroy, the challenger."

"Wait," said Grave, finally getting a grasp on the conversation. "According to Crab Cake Johnny, there was no security at all. If there were a threat, wouldn't there have been more security? Drones everywhere and so on?"

Morgan nodded at every point made by Grave. "Yes, yes, and they thought that they were at a high level of security. All their systems suggested scores of drones and other security equipment on the job. The fact of the matter, though, was that the bomber had disabled it all without them even being aware of it."

Snoot whistled through her teeth. "Wow."

"Indeed," said Morgan. "Indeed."

52

Pax didn't know what Sookie wanted, but she was giving him a strange look. "What?"

Sookie shook her head. "You know, you amaze me sometimes."

Pax smiled. "Thanks."

Sookie chuckled sardonically. "Oh, not in a *good* way, my boy."

Pax shrugged. "What's this all about? Why are you giving me that look?"

"You know, it's one thing to have a doctor for a girlfriend, but it's quite another when she's not aware of it."

Pax blanched. How could she know that? "But she will be, she will be."

Sookie rolled her eyes. "Really? You really believe that?"

"Yes, absolutely. I'm wearing her down."

"Oh, really? And how is that going?"

"Well, I think."

"Oh, and did you know she already had a boyfriend?"

Pax looked away. "Yeah, but I can handle the competition, whoever it is."

Sookie took out a cigarette, lit it, took a deep drag, and then let it out in one long puff, directly into Pax's face.

"Hey, quit it," he said, waving away the smoke.

Sookie stood and pointed a finger at him, her voice rising, angry. "Oh, I'll quit it, all right. Just as soon as you level with me."

Pax threw up his hands. "What's with you? I have leveled with you. Yeah, I really like Lara and I'm trying to get closer to her."

"And the boyfriend?"

Pax shrugged. "Mom, there's *always* another boyfriend with a woman like Lara. She's beautiful."

"Oh, she is that."

Pax startled. "Wait, you've seen her?"

Sookie nodded. "A while ago. She had good things to say about you. How attentive you were. How it was nice to have a friend like you, someone so empathetic."

Pax smiled. "She said that? See, she likes me."

"Oh, she does, son, but not in the way you're hoping—at least not yet, and definitely not *now*."

"Oh, and why's that?"

Sookie was incredulous. "You know, son. Don't tell me you don't know."

"Know? Know what?"

"About her boyfriend," she said, raising her eyebrows and holding them there, like battle flags. "The one and only *Superman*."

Pax's smile vanished, something darker taking its place.

A chill ran through Sookie. "What?"

Pax just shook his head, refusing to make eye contact.

Sookie steadied herself. "Oh, my god." She began pacing back and forth, trying to catch her breath. "You did it, didn't you? You *killed* him."

Pax shook his head, but tears were welling in his eyes.

53

There was even more to whistle about, at least to Charlize's way of thinking, and apparently to Morgan's as well, because he dutifully whistled through his teeth when Charlize laid out Plan B and her conversation with June.

"Holy crap," he added. "A backdoor to a backdoor."

"Yes, captain, and at least potentially, unauthorized access to every drone *and* simdroid in the world."

"So, Superman's drone and hovercycle are somewhere at the bottom of the bay."

Charlize nodded. "And I suppose a good number of the mayor's and the FBI's drones as well."

"Amazing."

"No, what's amazing, sir, is that Ramrod and the other manufacturers are totally aware of this and doing *nothing.*"

Morgan nodded. "Well, now we know."

Smithers raised his hand. "Sir, I think this is more serious than you know. We're not just talking about drones being deep-sixed, we're talking about an ability to influence every action of every drone and simdroid worldwide."

"Yes, of course. I realize that. But really, now that we know, maybe we can shut those backdoors." He turned to Blunt. "Maybe you could ask June."

"I already have," said Charlize. "And the process will take months, if not years. There are so many models, so many doorways."

"Sir," said Smithers, "if I might add to my concerns."

"Certainly."

"We have an election coming up, pitting a simdroid against a human for the first time."

"Yes, so?"

"What if someone is trying to manipulate the vote one way or the other?"

Grave, who had been in a deep funk ever since their five-minute coffee break, which had featured no coffee, and worse, a fresh Skunk 'n Donuts box featuring twelve chocolate stains where once a dozen chocolate donuts once sat proudly, suddenly perked up. "Maybe not just the vote, Smithers. If what Charlize says is true, even the *candidate* could be influenced. And if that's successful, we may find ourselves under the thumb of a simdroid mayor under the thumb of others."

Morgan chuckled. "You mean like with our human mayor?" The mayor's shady dealings with the Sons was well known within the department.

Grave shrugged. "Maybe worse, sir."

Morgan agreed. "Yeah, you're probably right about that. All right, so what now? We need proof. Has Lester Change been back-doored? And if so, by whom? And how does this fit with the bombing? And the murder?"

Charlize raised her hand. "Sir, if I may. Your questions suggest a grand scheme, but it has always been my feeling, and those of the other detectives programmed into me, that a grand scheme is often supported by baser emotions: greed, power, love, jealousy, and so on."

Morgan loved her skills but hated her long preambles. "Okay, so what's your point?"

"Motive, sir, motive. Who stands to gain from back-dooring Change? From bombing the mayor? From killing Superman?"

"Right, right," said Morgan. "But we don't even know if this back-dooring is even happening. How do we prove that?"

"Ah, a detail," said Smithers. "Charlize, do you remember?"

Charlize looked confused. "What?"

"I'm sure you were deep in thought, so maybe you didn't notice. As we left the Ramrod building, I observed a man in a heated conversation with the receptionist. He wanted to cancel Change's routine physical."

"Of course," said Charlize. "And the upshot was, he couldn't cancel. It was an election requirement."

"Exactly," said Smithers.

"Am I missing something?" said Morgan, shaking his head.

"I think what they're saying," said Grave, "is that we have an opportunity to see if Change has a backdoor, and if so, whether it has been opened."

"And by whom," said Charlize.

Morgan's eyes went wide. "Wonderful." He turned to Grave. "Grave, why don't you take Blunt and go check this out?"

Charlize, who rarely displayed emotions, was quick to do so now, leveling Morgan with an icy stare. "Sir, I must object." She turned to Grave. "No offense, Grave, but I think Smithers and I should continue on this line of investigation."

Grave turned to Morgan. "I have to agree, sir. As a simdroid herself, I think she is in a much better position to investigate this backdoor thing."

Morgan huffed once, indicating his displeasure at being challenged, but then forced a smile. "Very well, it's yours, Charlize."

"Thank you, sir. It's scheduled for first thing tomorrow morning, so we'll be on it."

"Good, good," said Morgan. "Now, assuming Change is under someone else's control, who would that be?"

Loblolly raised her hand. "Sir, I'm new to the force, but it seems to me that the only group that stands to gain from Change's election would be the Krypto Knights."

"That's possible, detective, but when it comes to political power as a motive, we can't rule out larger forces, perhaps even someone from the mainland."

Loblolly wasn't about to give up. "That may be, sir, but we can't rule out local forces, either. And we know the Krypto Knights are using back-dooring. You know, their Plan B."

"She has an excellent point, sir," said Charlize.

"She does indeed, sir," said Snoot, "and I'd like to volunteer the two of us to follow up with them. Keep the pressure on, so to speak."

"Okay, done," said Morgan. "Now, back to the murder. Who stands most to gain from killing Superman?"

"Well," said Blunt. "If we assume that the Krypto Knights are behind the back-dooring and perhaps the bombing, the likely candidate for the murder would be someone opposed to those ideas. Someone who stands to lose a great deal if the mayor were defeated, or killed."

Morgan had to admit that the cloud could sometimes be remarkably clear. "There are many groups that fit the bill. I've never seen the level of protesting we've seen over this new right of simdroids to vote and seek election."

"Yes, sir," said Blunt, "but you'd have to put the Sons of Irony at the top of that list."

Morgan didn't like the way this was going. The mayor would be furious with him if he even suggested the Sons were involved. Still, Blunt had a valid point. "True enough, Blunt, but they all seem to have alibis."

"Wait, sir," said Grave. "We never really pressed Claw's son on *his* whereabouts."

Morgan scoffed. "Well, he'll have an alibi, too. They'll make one up if they have to."

"Still," said Grave, "I'd like to keep them under pressure."

Morgan could see the mayor's face, but relented. "Very well, but don't force things." He turned to the others at the table. "All right, I think we know what everyone's going to do. Get out there and do your thing, and let's meet back here in the morning."

Everyone started pushing back their chairs, but a new voice was heard, one that had been silent throughout the resumed meeting. "Sir," said Horace the Seagull, "I'd like to help."

Morgan blinked like he had been unaware that Horace was even in the room. "What? How?"

"What would solve the case the fastest?"

Loblolly was quick to reply. "Well, for the murder, the FBI identifying the murderer's name on Superman's last phone call."

Horace cocked his head. "Yes, yes, but apart from that."

"That's easy," said Blunt. "Eye witnesses. But we have none. Whoever did this dismantled all the security and shut down the drones. Our only witness, Crab Cake Johnny, really saw very little. Certainly not enough to point the finger at anyone."

Horace shook his feathers. "Yes, well, there are witnesses and then there are witnesses. You have your disabled drones, I have the ear of every seagull in Crab Cove. And I'd bet a bucket of fries one or more of them saw the whole thing go down, from the bombing to the murder."

Morgan's mouth dropped open. "Well, then, what do you propose?"

"The obvious, sir. For another bucket of fries, I'll conduct my own investigation, find out what's really been going down." He got a faraway look in his eyes. "The answers are out there."

Morgan looked around the room. Everyone was nodding. "You do that, and you'll never want for fries again."

Horace beamed in the unique way any fry-scavenging gull would. "Sounds like a plan."

"And speaking of that," said Morgan, "let's change things up a bit. There's no sense pressuring the Sons or the Krypto Knights now if we have some hope that Horace here really can find some eye witnesses to the crimes. Besides, we'll know more about Change's backdoor, if it exists, by tomorrow morning. And there's every chance the FBI's technicians will be able to decipher the name of the killer on that call tape."

He took a deep breath. "So let's let Charlize and Horace do their work, and then we'll meet back here tomorrow. Charlize, what do you think? Say ten o'clock?"

"Yes, captain, that will work fine. We can be back here by then or give you a call."

"Okay then, folks, off you go."

Everyone started for the door, but then Morgan had another thought. "Wait a minute, wait a minute. Let's change this a little. Grave, you and Blunt pick up Pax tomorrow morning and bring him in for questioning. Nothing heavy-handed, mind. Just routine questioning." He turned to Snoot. "Snoot, you and Loblolly do the same. Pick up that Kent fellow and bring him in. Then, depending on what Charlize and Horace find, we can let them go or close this case down fast."

54

Claw was trying his best to control his anger, but Pax's persistence was beginning to get on his nerves. He glanced over at Sookie and could tell she was having the same problem. "Look, son, it doesn't matter a bushel of crabs what I think, or even what you did or didn't do."

Pax, sitting across from them at the club's meeting table, was tight-jawed in his opposition. "I won't do it. Period."

Claw sighed. "Are you seriously saying you won't even *try* to save yourself?"

"I'm not leaving."

Sookie slammed her hand down on the table. "Because of *her?* Sonny boy, that lady is in *grief*. She has no use for you now."

Pax turned his head away, refusing even to speak.

"Listen," said Claw. "Let me put it to you this way. You know that new remake of *The Godfather?*"

Pax snorted. "What?"

"Yeah, *The Godfather*. Remember, that character, what's his name?"

"Sonny," said Sookie.

"No," said Claw. "Sonny's the one who gets laser-gunned down. The other one."

"Michael?"

"Yeah, Michael. Anyway, so Michael kills those guys at the crab shack, and then Don Corleone sends him to Mars for a time, till everything blows over and it's safe for him to come back."

Pax was incredulous. "So I go to Mars and marry a nice Martian girl who gets blown up? Is that your idea?"

"No, no, don't be such a shithead. What I'm saying is that you go to Mars, yeah, but it will serve two purposes. First, it gets you the hell away from Detective Grave and the others. And second, you'll be working with The Craters to set up franchises for our crab trucks up there."

Pax scoffed. "The Craters? I thought you said we'd never work with them."

"Because of the drugs, yeah. But things are different now, and besides, we can't keep smuggling crabs to Mars forever. This will give us a shot at going legit up there. And the money should be great." He sighed. "And if you're going to take over this club one day, Mars will be the key to everything, let me tell you."

"I don't know. If I go, the cops will see this as running, and I've told you, I have no reason to run. I didn't do anything."

"Pax, Pax, Pax, are we back at that again? Listen, the mayor can only help us so far. The media is clamoring for a resolution to the bombing and the murder, and there's only a small window of time before the mayor will start pressuring me."

"What, you'd give me up?"

"No, of course not. But here's the thing. What happens with the investigation is out of my control—out of *your* control—if you stay. But if you go. Well, son, there's no extradition treaty on Mars. Whether you done it or not, you'll be safe."

Pax looked back and forth between them. "But what about Lara? I'll lose her for sure."

Sookie used her there-there voice, the one she'd been using on Pax his whole life when he got into trouble. "Honey, you don't have her now. She needs time, too. So tell you what. You go to Mars and leave Lara to me. "I'll check in on her, keep your name in the conversation, talk you up while you're gone. She could use some mothering right about now, and I can do that for you, honey."

Pax let out a long sigh, then nodded. "Okay, okay, when do I leave?"

"Tomorrow, first thing," said Claw, relieved. "And first class."

The Reverend Bendigo Bottoms, late of this world, but still going strong at the Crab Cove Cinema Cemetery, slapped his knees and gave out with a deep belly laugh that seemed to echo throughout the cemetery. "A seagull, you say? A *talking* seagull?"

Grave knew it sounded ridiculous, but the reverend, one of only two ghosts Grave could see so far, seemed curious about the case, so he had filled him in. "I know, I know."

The reverend tried to control himself, but began laughing even harder. He could barely get out his next words. "What's next? A lineup? A seagull picking out the murderer from a lineup?"

Grave hadn't thought about that. It *was* ridiculous. "No, I'm sure it will all come to nothing. Horace will do anything for French fries, so I suspect he'll come back with a story of some sort, but nothing more."

The reverend took a deep breath, or at least went through the motions of taking a deep breath, his need for oxygen understandably far, far below that for the living. "Still, a talking seagull. That's really something. Do you suppose I could meet him one day?"

Grave shrugged. "I guess. He'll pretty much do anything for a bucket of French fries."

"Good, good." The reverend suddenly turned somber. "Can I ask you something else?"

"Jeez, why the look, reverend?"

The reverend sighed. "When I saw you walking up the path to greet me, I saw a lonely man, a sad man. What gives with you?"

Now it was Grave's turn to sigh. "I don't know. You once told me that life was like a tuna fish sandwich."

"I did, I did indeed. And, of course, it is."

"Right, right, no question about it. And then, when I asked you about death, and what that was like, you said it was quite the entrée."

The reverend spread out his arms. "Look around. It is."

"Yes, yes, I get that."

The reverend frowned. "Simon, where are you going with this?"

Grave shook his head. "I don't know. Every day seems to be the same old same old, if you know what I mean."

The reverend took a step back and looked him up and down. And then his eyes grew wide. "Oh, oh. Son, when was the last time you got laid?"

Grave turned away. "No, that's not what I'm talking about."

"Yes, it is."

"No, it isn't."

The reverend shook his head. "Well, it's *part* of it at least."

Grave sighed. He had to admit it was. "Yeah, I guess, but it's more than that."

The reverend nodded knowingly. "It's love, isn't it? You miss love. You need love."

Grave chuckled, but it had a sardonic edge to it. "Well, a *date* would be a good start."

"Well, then, *ask* someone why don't you?"

"Yeah, but who?"

The reverend crossed his arms and gave Grave a good long look. "You're what, mid-forties?"

"Yeah, so?"

"Nothing. Just trying to get a likely age range for you. For a date, that is. So tell me, when was the last time you asked someone for a date?"

Grave remembered it well. He had seen a beautiful young woman at Le Crabe Bleu and had used his drone Barry to actually make the ask. "A few weeks ago."

The reverend nodded. "Good, so not too long ago. And tell me, how old was this woman?"

Grave's hem had a haw in it. "Well, um, you know, she was, um, young."

"How young?"

"Eighteen."

The reverend laughed. "Eighteen? Are you kidding me? And let me guess, she turned you down."

"Flat."

"Yep, just as I suspected. Simon, Simon, Simon, you need to set your sights on someone a little older. An 18-year-old's skin is on way too tight for a man your age. No, you need a woman with a little more experience."

"So, someone with *loose* skin?"

"Simon, don't make fun of me. I'm just saying you're fishing in the wrong pond."

"All right, all right."

The reverend stroked his chin. "Let's try this. Simon, close your eyes."

"What?"

"Close your eyes. This will work. Trust me."

Grave closed his eyes.

"Now," said the reverend. "Just think of a woman."

Grave's eyes popped open.

"What?" said the reverend.

"A woman, I thought of a woman."

"Wonderful, wonderful. And who was this woman?"

Grave shook his head, tight-lipped.

"Oh, come on, Simon. You won't even tell a dead man?"

Grave relented. "Okay, okay, she's a colleague, a detective new to the force."

The reverend smiled. "So, what's the problem? Ask her out."

Grave ran his hand through his hair. "I don't know. She really hasn't shown much interest in me. And whether she says yes or no, it would change our professional relationship forever."

The reverend tried his best to make a tch-tch-tch sound, but it came out more like a sputter. "Simon, if this is how you approach things, you'll never get laid."

Grave raised an eyebrow. "Whatever."

The reverend just glowered at Grave until Grave couldn't stand it anymore. "What?"

"Are you *sure* she isn't interested?"

Grave thought about it. There had been a few glances, a few shared smiles, but he put those down to her being new and wanting to fit in. "Um, maybe."

The reverend clapped his hands. "Oh, I do so love the word *maybe*. It means you're open to *yes*."

"I guess."

The reverend threw his arm around Grave's shoulders. "Look, going forward, pay more attention to her. Look for signs of attraction."

"Such as?"

"I don't know. You know her better than I do. Glances, smiles, perhaps a seemingly accidental touch. You know, when I first touched my hand to my wife's, it was like being struck by lightning."

Grave chuckled. "All right."

The reverend smiled broadly. "Excellent, my boy. Just look for a sign."

Grave nodded.

The reverend chuckled, seemingly over nothing.

"What now?"

The reverend pointed at the balloons on his grave stone. "In all this time, you haven't once mentioned my birthday balloons, or the stickers and glitter all over my stone."

Grave glanced at the balloons. There were three of them and each bore the likeness of the reverend, drawn with a marker. "Looks just like you."

"I know, she's quite the artist."

"Who?"

The reverend seemed surprised. "What, you haven't met Nancy?"

Grave remembered Victoria talking about her. "The new arrival, you mean?"

"Yes, yes, the sweetest person you're likely to meet, alive or dead."

"Victoria mentioned something about her, but I'm not even sure if I could see her if I saw her. Um, so to speak."

The reverend clapped his hands. "A delight. A pure delight. You can't miss her. She is tall and has gray hair, done up in almost a Friar Tuck hairdo." He laughed. "And she's covered in glitter and stickers, just like my stone here."

"Well," said Grave, not sure what to say.

"Go, go now, she's over at Victoria's bench. They meet every evening at this time to go over who's next on the balloon list."

"Birthday balloons."

"Oh, come on, Simon. Think about it. Cemeteries are all about birthdays. Why, they're even carved in our stones so no one will forget."

Grave chuckled. "I guess. Okay, I'll go meet her. Nice talking to you."

"You, too, Simon. And don't forget, look for a sign."

And with that, the late Reverend Bendigo Bottoms disappeared.

56

Charlize and Smithers sat behind the control panel next to the cloud that was June Thursday, along with a control technician named Blake, who seemed to have a penchant for sucking his teeth in response to the patterns of flashing lights on the console. The control room was like all the other rooms at Ramrod Robotics, a distortion of space and reality, the wet dream of an unfettered architect who thought mating triangles and trapezoids was just the right thing to do. As a result, no matter which way you looked, the room seemed to be simultaneously rising to meet you as it fell away. It was disorienting and dizzying.

Before them, through a large plate glass window, they could see the examination floor, where Lester Change was being examined. Technicians in baby blue clean-suits swarmed around the simdroid, checking this and that.

The whole scene made Charlize cringe. She knew full well what it was like to be led into that room for her annual physical. They would take you to the center of the room, to an examination station that looked more like a torture device than the techno-medical marvel that it was. Every time she went in, she would focus on the people in the control room looking out at her and wonder what they were thinking. That lasted but moments as a technician pulled out the simcortex from her back, the device that controlled and defined everything Charlize.

"Okay," said June, "the simcortex is out. We should have some data momentarily."

Charlize stared at the now slumped over Lester Change. "He's an odd duck, isn't he?"

"How so?" said June.

"He looks like an idiot."

"No," said Smithers. "I've had the same feeling for a while now, so I ran an image of him against other historical images in my database."

"And?" said Charlize.

"Strangely, I came up with two rather close matches."

"Go on," said June.

"Well, the first is a cartoon character in an old humor periodical called *Mad Magazine*. The character is called Alfred E. Neuman." He stopped and looked around at the monitors that lined the walls. "Here, I'll send it to monitor four there."

The image popped up on the screen, and June laughed out loud. "Oh, that's priceless. Not perfect of course, but there's something about his eyes and that silly grin."

"Indeed, yes," said Smithers. "Now, I'm not sure you'll recognize this next image, because it goes back a hundred years to a television show called *The Howdy Doody Show*."

When the image came up, June nearly fell on the floor, laughing. "Oh, that's even better."

Charlize shook her head. "Idiotic, right? Why would anyone pick Ronald Reagan for the first simdroid politician? I just don't get it."

June nodded. "Right, I see what you're saying, but I sat in on the early discussions. There was a lot of support for George Washington and Lincoln, of course, but they were judged to be too old and too hallowed for a mayoral run. And everyone balked at any notion of Nixon or Trump. Anyway, I was pulled from the room at that point to deal with a personnel problem, and by the time I got back, the selection had been made."

"I still don't get it," said Charlize.

"Hmm, well, the explanation given me was that Ronald Reagan had just the right qualities to match Mayor Bancroft's affability and cunning."

"Okay," said Charlize. "Now *that* makes sense." She looked down at the control panel, which had begun to flash lights in a more dramatic way than previously. "What's this?"

The technician, Blake, spun on his chair, sucked at his teeth, and pushed at several buttons on the console. "Coming up."

Data began streaming on the console's monitor, too fast even for Charlize or Smithers to follow, but not apparently for the tooth-sucking Blake. "Normal, normal, normal." He turned to Charlize and shook his head. "Nothing to see here. Every trait and capability checks out. Intelligence, reasoning, speed, honesty, adherence to the Laws of Robotics—*everything* is pegged at ten out of ten, the highest level."

Charlize frowned. "Are you sure?"

Blake pointed at the data frozen on the screen. "Data are data."

Charlize sighed. "Do me a favor and look again. We're looking for any sort of backdoor, some way of tampering with his simcortex."

Blake sucked on his teeth, turned back to the screen, and began scrolling through the data stream again, this time more slowly. "Nothing, nothing, nothing, *whoa*—what's this?"

He abruptly stopped the stream of data and pointed at a string of characters on the monitor. "That's not right. That code shouldn't be there."

Charlize leaned in and looked at the screen. "What's up?"

"The simcortex has been corrupted."

"A backdoor?" said Charlize.

"Yes," said Blake, pointing at the screen and sucking on his teeth with a force that would have impressed a Robovacuum 3000. "See here, that little string."

Smithers looked as well. "That's it? That's all it takes?"

"Apparently," said June. She turned to Blake. "Can you open it?"

Blake squinted at the screen as if it would give him the key to the backdoor. "It's not very sophisticated. In fact, it's so simple, it's sublime. Short and sweet code, easily missed. Here, let me give this a try." He clacked away at the keys and a new window opened up on the screen. "Ha, we're in."

"Great," said Charlize. "Can you tell me what's been changed?"

June wondered whether Blake could do so without sucking his teeth, but she was deeply disappointed.

"Yes," he said, scanning the coding. Reasoning is at ten, as well as intelligence and speed—that's all good. But, oh my, honesty is at three and resistance to greed and lawlessness are at a rock-bottom zero."

"Lawlessness?" said Charlize. "Do you mean the rule of law or the Laws of Robotics?"

Blake sucked his teeth, hard. "Both."

"So now what?" said Smithers. "Can we change the settings back to what they should be?"

Blake turned and clacked away at the keyboard, then stopped to suck his teeth. He clacked away again, and then turned back to them. "It's not responding to my commands. We're blocked."

June was as incredulous as she was stratocumulus. "Surely there's a way to set this right."

Blake shook his head emphatically and crossed his arms, leaving teeth-sucking for another time. "Nope."

Another time came quickly, the suckless silence ending explosively. A sudden burst of sparks directed their attention back to the laboratory floor. Lester Change's simcortex was self-destructing, smoke and sparks and flames rising from it and the simcortex analyzer.

Blake would later say it made a distinctive sucking noise before it died.

57

Grave was late to the station, and he didn't much care. He had been in an absolute funk ever since his conversation with Reverend Bottoms. Look for a sign, the man had said. And since then, that is what Grave had been doing. Street signs, stop signs, business signs, and all those political signs touting Bancroft and Change, but no sign of love, affection, or even mild interest.

Grave pulled into the parking lot, the Sprite's radio suddenly dropping from its usual full-on setting of eleven, the sound of gospel music reverberating throughout the community, to the zero of silence. He could see the cloud that was Blunt waiting for him next to their police hovercruiser. But there was something about the cloud that suggested that Blunt was not upset at all at Grave's tardiness. Something was up, but what?

Grave climbed out of the Sprite, which was comical for a man his size with a car so small, and stepped on something—something soft. As he had climbed out, a bag of some kind had fallen out with him. When he looked down and saw a skunk looking back at him, he knew exactly what it was: a takeout bag from Skunk 'n Donuts, and what lay inside could only be a donut.

He picked up the bag and looked closer. Someone had drawn a little heart next to the skunk's head. A chill went through Grave. Could this be the sign?

As he considered this, Blunt rushed up to him. "Where have you been? It's all going down."

Grave broke his reverie over the bag and tossed it back into the Sprite. "Wait, what?"

"Morgan had a brainstorm, pulled in everyone early for a lineup."

"What? I thought we were supposed to pick up Pax."

"He's already here, along with Claw. They were on their way to the Mars Terminal, if you can believe it."

"Really?"

"Yeah, in full flight, apparently."

"Wow."

"You can say that again. And Morgan's also brought in people from all the other gangs."

"But the Vie Kings and the SanniClaws really aren't suspects."

"Right, right. Morgan thinks by bringing them all in, the real suspects will think we're just fishing."

"So he's trying to put them off balance, then."

"Yep."

"Interesting move. So, did Charlize or Horace find anything?"

Blunt laughed. "Oh, yeah. Our mayor want-to-be has been hacked, and Horace has produced two eye witnesses."

"Wow."

"Exactly. Come on, we don't want to miss this."

Grave followed Blunt into the station, which appeared to be more like a three-ring circus than a professional police squad room. In one ring were all the suspects: Claw and Pax from the Sons; Kent Abrams from the Krypto Knights; Bluetooth Mortenson and Pokie Sigurdsen from the Vie Kings; and Brush Langley and Mr. Bucket Furlong from the SanniClaws. In a second ring there were officers at the coffee bot, scrambling for donuts. And in the third ring, there was Detective Snoot, putting her new personal drone through a series of dizzying acrobatic loops around the room.

And in a fourth ring—this was clearly way beyond anything a three-ring circus could offer—was a small group of Grave's fellow detectives, motioning him forward.

"It's about time," said Morgan. "Wouldn't want to miss this, Grave."

"So I hear," said Grave. He turned to Charlize and Horace. "I hear you've been busy."

Charlize smiled at him, but it was a smile coming from behind her that Grave was locked on. He wasn't sure what kind of smile it was, but it was clearly meant for him, and it came from a woman clearly capable of drawing a heart on a takeout bag: Detective Polly Loblolly.

Charlize brought him back to the moment. "We found the backdoor."

"And I found two witnesses," said Horace, ruffling his feathers with a full amount of pride.

Grave nodded and looked back over Charlize's shoulder. Loblolly's smile had faded, but he still detected interest in her eyes. Um, maybe.

But now Morgan had him by the elbow. "Come on, let's get this show on the road." He turned to Blunt. "Get them all in the lineup room."

"Yes, sir."

Morgan turned back to Grave. "Let's get to the viewing room, so I can introduce you to our witnesses."

Grave followed Morgan and the others across the squad room and into the room next to the lineup room, where they could watch the suspects through a mirrored wall.

Two seagulls were waiting for them, each with a bucket of fries in front of them, which they seemed to be enjoying immensely.

Horace squawked at them, and they immediately stopped gobbling French fries. He squawked again and they squawked back. There was nothing in their volume or tone that suggested anything more intelligent than a squawk, but Horace turned back to the group and seemed to be beaming. "They're ready."

Morgan turned and pressed an intercom button on the wall. "Blunt, bring them in."

A cloud suddenly appeared on the other side of the mirror, followed by Claw, Pax, Bluetooth, Pokie, Kent, Brush, and Mr. Bucket, each with a numbered sign on his chest from one to seven.

This is certainly no Magnificent Seven, thought Grave. *More like the Malfeasant Seven.*

Morgan turned to the gulls, Horace translating. "Take your time, as much time as you need. Do you recognize any of these men?"

Both gulls began squawking at once.

Horace squawked back at them, and the squawking continued for some seconds. Finally, Horace held up a wing to silence them, and turned to Morgan. "Charlie here says he recognizes Suspect Two."

Morgan nodded. "Okay, let's make sure." He pushed the button on the intercom. "Number Two, please step forward."

Pax, startled, stepped forward, trying to force a smile, like this was all some joke.

"Is that the man?" said Horace.

Charlie squawked and bobbed his head.

"He says yes."

Morgan turned back to the intercom. "Number Two, step back."

Pax dutifully complied, giving Claw a reassuring smile.

Morgan turned back to Horace once more. "What about your other friend? Did he see anything?"

Horace bobbed his head. "Yes, and she's a she."

"Sorry."

"No problem, happens all the time." Horace turned and seemed to wink at Vivian, the other gull. "Vivian wants to take a closer look at Number Five."

When Number Five, Kent, stepped forward, Vivian began squawking again.

"That's him," said Horace. "She's certain."

Morgan smiled broadly. "Excellent." He activated the intercom once more. "Blunt, take numbers two and five to interview rooms one and two. The others may go."

Grave watched for Pax's and Kent's reactions, but both were expressionless. Claw, on the other hand, was livid, and began pushing Pax toward the door, shouting something at him. Then he turned, rushed the mirror, and began pounding on it several times before Blunt was able to wrestle him away.

Whatever was said was lost to everyone on Grave's side of the mirror, but Blunt must have heard it.

Grave turned back to Horace.

"So what exactly did Charlie and Vivian see?"

Horace shook his head. "Not so fast. First, more French fries all around."

58

What seagulls Charlie and Vivian had seen was both encouraging and maddening. Charlie had been perched high atop a light pole in the Crab Cove Hospital's parking lot, trying to get some sleep when the sound of a heated argument awakened him. Two men, each in different cuts, were scuffling below. According to Charlie, Pax was certainly one of them. He didn't get a good look at the other man, so he couldn't say for sure whether he had been in the lineup.

Vivian had also been sleeping when a fight erupted below her. In her case, she had selected a beam under the debate stage to spend the night. She was on the outs with her boyfriend, and knew he'd never find her there. The scene below her was only lit by a couple of flashlights, so her view of the action was limited. What she was sure about was that Kent was stabbing another man in the back repeatedly. It was all over in seconds, and then the lights went out. From her spot, she could hear one man move away, and then minutes later, the other man moaned and also moved away.

"Well," said Captain Morgan, scratching his head, "I don't know about the rest of you, but my money's on Vivian. It's Kent we're after."

"I don't know," said Grave. "Two things trouble me about that."

"Oh?"

"For starters, according to Vivian, the murder scene was dimly lit. Could she really positively identify Kent under those conditions, or was she just seeing two men in cuts?"

"A fair point," said Morgan. "I'll give you that."

"And," said Grave, "we know Superman chose to die in the clubhouse of the Sons. Why would he do that if Pax wasn't his killer?"

Charlize jumped in. "Both reasonable objections, Grave, but I think we'll find in the end that Vivian did indeed see Kent murder Superman. And I think we'll find that Charlie's story, though perhaps true, was tangential to the crime. Some personal beef between two men."

"Then why did Superman go to the Sons?"

Charlize pursed her lips. "I admit that's a head scratcher, but look at it from Superman's perspective. He knows he's dying and knows he'll never make it to the hospital in time. The Sons clubhouse is right there in front of him, and there's really no serious disagreement between the clubs—they even do a good business in burner drones—so he stops there, his last hope for help."

Grave sighed. "That could work. But what would Kent's motive be?"

Snoot, who had been as quiet as Loblolly during the discussion, piped up. "We're talking about hovercycle clubs, folks. Power struggles abound. Not unusual at all for a number two to take down his number one."

"I agree," said Charlize. "And it may have something to do with the bombing, a disagreement perhaps."

"Okay," said Grave. "You're theory could work."

Morgan was nodding vigorously. "Yes, I think Kent's our man, too, but I have a third theory."

Grave and Charlize looked at him, bewildered. "Sir?" they said, almost simultaneously.

"My theory is that whichever theory is correct, the DA isn't going to pursue either one based on the eye-witness testimony of seagulls."

Everyone agreed the captain had a fair point. They would need a confession. Nothing else would do.

59

After some dickering about who would interrogate whom, Morgan decided to let Grave and Blunt tackle Pax while Charlize and Smithers went after Kent.

From the beginning, it was clear that they had made a tactical error in having both men in the same lineup. For the first hour, the most common phrase in each room was, *it wasn't me; it must be him*. Kent wasn't admitting to anything: to being at the debate stage, to setting the bombs, to killing Superman. On the other hand, he had no alibi other than convenient insomnia. He had been out riding around on his hovercycle, he said. And his drone had conveniently gone missing, the result, Charlize surmised, of Plan B.

Pax was equally slippery at first, but then admitted scuffling with Superman in the hospital parking lot, over a woman, whom he wouldn't say. He, too, made a claim of riding around all night, not from insomnia, but as a way of calming down after a heated argument. Yes, he had pursued Superman briefly, hoping to continue the argument, but then had broken off the pursuit as his anger subsided. He'd ended up at the beach to watch the sunrise. He had nothing to do with the bombs or the murder, and when pressed about his trip to Mars, claimed it was for "good and sound" business reasons, and nothing more.

By the second hour, neither Charlize nor Grave had put a dent in either man's story. Both men's stances continued to be, "You've got nothing on me, copper!"

"Why don't we switch it up, then," said Morgan during a break. "Charlize, you take Pax. Grave, go at Kent. Maybe that will trip one of them up."

But after another two hours it was clear that sometimes even good ideas don't pan out. Neither man was budging from his story.

Morgan was disheartened to say the least, images of an angry mayor and a livid DA dancing not just in his head, but on it. "What now?" he said, looking woebegone.

No one said anything. The captain had assembled them all in the conference room, hoping for ideas that would move the interrogations forward to a confession by one man or the other. But the silence spoke volumes about the entire team's frustration.

And then, out of the blue, Grave started laughing. It began as a snort, followed by a titter that led to a giggle, a snicker, a chortle, and an outright guffaw.

"What?" said Morgan.

"Oh, sir," said Grave, trying his best to stifle his laugh. "I know *exactly* what we must do."

***

Twenty minutes later, as Kent sat twiddling his thumbs in the interrogation room, the door swung open with a bang. A tall woman with close-cropped blond hair strode in, her eyes fixed on Kent.

Kent sat up in his chair. "Who the hell are you?"

The woman came up to the table and sat down calmly opposite him. There was an icy look about her, and Kent was almost certain he recognized her, but from where, he wasn't certain.

"My name is Retective Tilda Must."

Something about her voice, the steel in it, made him gulp.

Epilogue

A week later, on the day after the election, Detectives Snoot and Loblolly sat at a long picnic table outside Bob's House of Crabs, hammering away at crabs steamed in Old Bay.

"It's hard to believe," said Loblolly.

"What do you mean?"

"Everything. Tilda. Kent." She paused to chuckle. "The election."

Snoot laughed with her. "So now we have a simdroid mayor. Who'd a thunk it?"

"Or any of it, for that matter."

Snoot scoffed. "Oh, I knew it was Kent all along, and Tilda just nailed him. Grave, for once, had a good idea."

"You were right about Kent. He wanted to be president of the club, and to control Lester Change."

"Yeah, it all fell into place. Kent wanted to bomb the debate, but Superman didn't, and when Superman showed up to make sure no bombs had been set, Kent jumped him."

Loblolly started to slam her mallet into an unsuspecting crab claw but stopped, the mallet poised in the air. "But the mystery still remains. Why did Superman go to the Sons?"

Snoot shrugged. "Dunno. Maybe he really didn't see who had stabbed him. He'd had the fight with Pax earlier, so that would have been on his mind. Dying on their doorstep could have been his way of implicating Pax. And a bit of irony for the Sons of Irony.

Loblolly shook her head. "I don't know if *that's* irony, but it's surely ironic that Superman's death was by a Krypto Knight."

Snoot thought for a second, then threw her head back. "Ha!"

Loblolly looked around at the other tables, which were full up with people slamming away at crabs. "Can I ask you something?"

Snoot lowered her mallet. "Sure, shoot."

"What gives with Simon? He's said nothing about the chocolate donut I left in his car."

Snoot rolled her eyes. "There's no telling with that man. Just give it time."

"But I drew a heart on the bag. What couldn't he understand about that?"

Snoot shook her head. "Men. Sometimes they just can't read the signs."

Loblolly frowned, then slammed her mallet into the back of a whole crab. "Shit!"

***

Across town, in Sergeant Blunt's and June's garage, Rippley was performing her magic before a crowd of visible children, all students in her new school of casual invisibility. She said the words and made the motions, and slowly, ever so slowly, the clouds that were her father and mother began to appear. First they were high cirrocumulus clouds, but Rippley made another wave of her hands and they became mid-level nimbostratus clouds. A few more waves of her arms, and the clouds became low-level cumulonimbus clouds. And then, with a sweep of her arms and a shout, Barry and June appeared to the children, fully visible for the first times in their lives. The children screamed.

***

At the Crab Cove Cinema Cemetery, Simon thought to scream, he was so frustrated. "I don't know what to make of it, reverend. She gave me a donut, but since then she's been standoffish, a complete mystery."

"Women *are* that, son," said the reverend. "But it's surely a *sign*."

"You think?"

"Son, when a woman draws a little heart on a bag containing a chocolate donut, well, that is *ipso facto* a sign."

"Are you sure?"

"Son, son, son, it's like I always say, *Love is like a chocolate donut.*"

Simon wanted to believe him. The reverend had been right about life being like a tuna fish sandwich. And Simon was sure the reverend was in a better position than he was to say that death was like an entrée, but was he right about love? Could love really be as simple as that?

Love, the maker, breaker, and destroyer of hearts. Love, the healer. Love, the berserker. Love, everlasting. Love won. Love lost. Love unrequited. Love, the plaything of poets. Love, by the sonnet. The joy of Love. The pain of Love. Love, the ninth potion. Love, it's all we need. Love, Love, Love.

All these thoughts—and more—should have been swirling in Grave's mind. How could a hole surrounded by fried dough and dipped in sweet chocolate encompass all that was Love? And could even a blind man see a chocolate donut?

And yet, the only thought in Grave's mind was this:

"Wait, no sprinkles?"

Note From The Author

Word-of-mouth is crucial for any author to succeed. If you enjoyed *Simon Grave and the Sons of Irony,* please leave a review online—anywhere you are able. Even if it's just a sentence or two. It would make all the difference and would be very much appreciated.

Thanks!
Len

About the Author

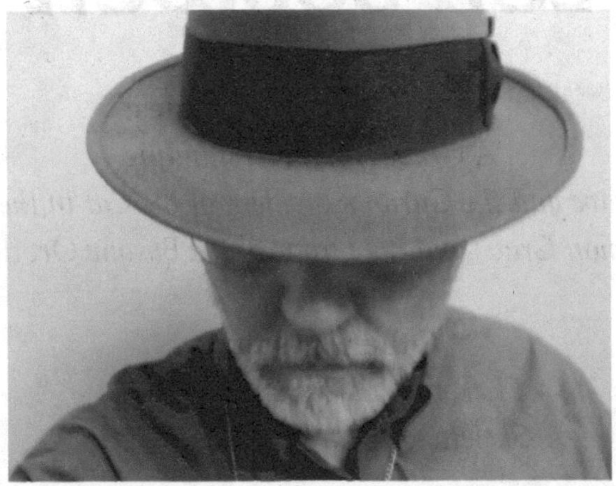

Len Boswell is the author of seven additional books, including *Simon Grave and the Curious Incident of the Cat in the Daytime, Simon Grave and the Drone of the Basque Orvilles, A Grave Misunderstanding, Flicker: A Paranormal Mystery, Skeleton: A Bare Bones Mystery, The Leadership Secrets of Squirrels,* and *Santa Takes a Tumble.* He lives in the mountains of West Virginia with his wife, Ruth, and their two dogs, Shadow and Cinder.

Other books by Len Boswell

Simon Grave Mysteries:

A Grave Misunderstanding

Simon Grave and the Curious Incident of the Cat in the Daytime

Simon Grave and the Drone of the Basque Orvilles

Other Mysteries:

Flicker: A Paranormal Mystery

Skeleton: A Bare Bones Mystery

Memoirs:

Santa Takes a Tumble

Nonfiction:

The Leadership Secrets of Squirrels

Stick Figures: The Life and Art of Len Boswell

Thank you so much for reading one of **Len Boswell's** novels.

If you enjoyed this book, please check out our recommendation for your next great read!

A Grave Misunderstanding by Len Boswell

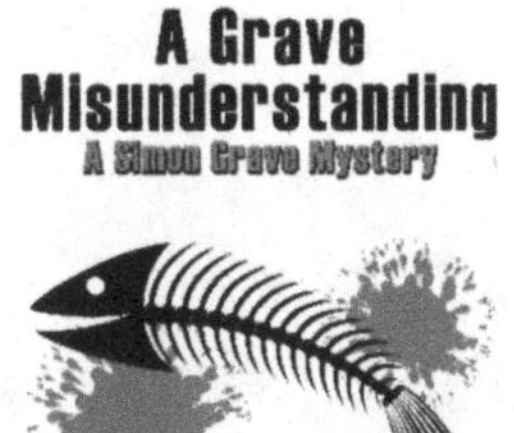

"The Bottom Line: A truly hilarious mystery in the tradition of Janet Evanovich, Thomas Davidson and Rich Leder."

-Best Thrillers

www.ingramcontent.com/pod-product-compliance
Lightning Source LLC
Chambersburg PA
CBHW011136100726
47898CB00009B/3001

* 9 7 8 1 6 8 4 3 3 6 2 1 0 *